"Are you sure we're going to meet *that* many guys?" Holly wasn't quite convinced.

"Are you joking? We are, definitely. I mean, for sure we'll meet more than we did last summer — what were we doing again?" Ainslee tapped the side of her head. "Oh, yeah. Now I remember. *Nothing*. For *weeks*."

"But we're going to be too busy working this year to hang out just looking for guys," Holly said.

"Working? Come on. I'll be playing tennis occasionally. You'll be pouring sodas. That's only thirty or forty hours a week. That leaves us plenty of time to socialize. And by socialize? I mean flirt."

"There's just one problem. Do we know how to flirt?" Holly asked.

Ainslee laughed. "Not well. But we'll learn."

i ❤ bikinis

He's With Me by Tamara Summers

Island Summer by Jeanine Le Ny

What's Hot by Caitlyn Davis

What's
Hot

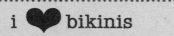

i ♥ bikinis

What's Hot

Caitlyn Davis

Point

No part of this work may be reproduced, stored in a retrieval system, or transmitted in any form or by any means, electronic, mechanical, photocopying, recording, or otherwise, without written permission of the publisher. For information regarding permission, write to Scholastic Inc., Attention: Permissions Department, 557 Broadway, New York, NY 10012.

ISBN-13: 978-0-439-91852-7
ISBN-10: 0-439-91852-9

Copyright © 2007 by Catherine Clark

SCHOLASTIC, POINT, and associated logos are trademarks and/or registered trademarks of Scholastic Inc.

12 11 10 9 8 7 6 5 4 3 2 1   7 8 9 10 11 12/0

Printed in the U.S.A.   01
First printing, July 2007

What's
Hot

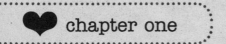

"I love guys who wear flip-flops."

Holly Bannon watched a guy amble across the large lawn at Mrs. Whittingham's estate, where she and her best friend, Ainslee, were attending a "Welcome to the Club" party. They were both working at the Ridgemont Country Club for the summer, starting the next day.

"I don't know. Isn't he a little short for you?" Holly asked Ainslee, who was nearly 5' 9".

"Crudités?" A caterer holding a tray paused in front of them.

"Sorry?" Holly asked.

"It's an appetizer," Ainslee said. "Take one. Très delicious." She grabbed one from the tray and popped it into her mouth.

"Thanks," Holly told the caterer. She carefully took a small bite of the celery, nibbling the edge. She watched as another guy jogged across the lawn, toward the shuffleboard court on the other side of the inground pool.

Shuffleboard, thought Holly. *Who ever even heard of it before tonight?*

"How about him, Ains?" she asked.

"Mmm . . . no." Ainslee shook her head. "Don't like the hat."

"Really?" Holly took another look at him. "You're too picky. I think he's cute. Or he was, but I can't really see him anymore."

"He's all right, but I hate the way he runs. Anyway. We're going to meet so many guys this summer. We don't have to settle for someone who's just sort of okay and wears a baseball cap sideways," Ainslee declared. "My mom always says never settle."

Holly wasn't quite convinced. "Are you sure we're going to meet *that* many guys?" It wasn't as if the Ridgemont Country Club was strictly for high-school guys. *Although that would be cool*, she thought. Except then she couldn't belong to it, which wouldn't be cool at all.

"Are you joking? We are, definitely. I mean, for sure we'll meet more than we did last summer — what were we doing again?" Ainslee tapped the

2

side of her head. "Oh yeah. Now I remember. *Nothing*. For *weeks*."

"But we're going to be too busy working this year to hang out just looking for guys," Holly said.

"Working? Come on. I'll be playing tennis occasionally. You'll be pouring sodas. That's only thirty or forty hours a week. That leaves us plenty of time to socialize. And by socialize? I mean flirt."

"There's just one problem. Do we know how to flirt?" Holly asked.

Ainslee laughed. "Not well. But we'll learn."

Holly had to admit that they'd both scored in getting jobs at Ridgemont for the summer. It was the best place to work, because students from all around the area were hired as staff. It was a chance to hang out with a big crowd, and meet some-one new, and there were lots of parties over the summer, too. Also, the club's owner, Mrs. Whittingham, believed in letting employees have access to the gym, the golf course, the tennis courts — and most important to Holly, the pool.

But the club wasn't without its problems: one, the fact that it hadn't been updated in thirty years and looked a little run-down, and two, the fact that Mrs. Whittingham didn't seem to notice that the courts needed resurfacing, the golf course had grown shaggy, and half of the gym lockers had broken locks.

Three, the fact that the official club lemonade tasted very, very strange, and no one seemed to notice *that*, either.

"Come on, let's go over there and check things out," Ainslee said.

A couple of small dogs were racing around the expansive lawn, and there was a group of guys gathered on the shuffleboard court.

"This lemonade tastes weird, doesn't it?" Holly asked as they wandered around.

"It's too sour, that's all," Ainslee said.

Holly stopped and leaned against a hedge, trying to look casual as they surveyed the shuffleboard court. "Do you see that guy with the dark blue T-shirt?" she asked Ainslee. "He looks familiar." Holly felt like she knew him from somewhere else, but she couldn't imagine where. Was he one of her sisters' ex-boyfriends? But he looked too young for that.

"He doesn't look familiar, but I wish he did," Ainslee said. "He's hot. You know, he looks like your type. Kind of a jock, but kind of more interesting than that."

"I didn't know I had a type. Well, we know one thing. He definitely doesn't go to East," Holly said.

"No. Our school's big, but not that big. We'd know about him," Ainslee said. "Maybe we met him at the club on our tour or when we were interviewing?"

"Maybe. But I think we'd remember," Holly said. *At least, I know I would have.*

"True. You know what? We should try to meet him tonight. Go pretend to push him into the water or something," Ainslee suggested. "Or just, like, bump into him." She tapped her finger against her chin, thinking. "I know! Spill something on him."

"Oh, yeah, he'll love that," Holly said. "Ains, where do you get these ideas? Honestly."

"Magazines, mostly." Ainslee sipped her lemonade. "And my mom."

"Your *mom*? Not again. Are you serious?" *This couldn't be good,* Holly thought.

"She's been dating a lot lately," Ainslee said. Her parents had divorced about three years carlier, when Ainslee was just starting junior high.

She'd barely forgiven them, since it wasn't the most fun year she'd ever had. She tended to sound jaded as a result.

"Still. Why would you take her advice?" Holly asked. "Does she know how impossible it is to meet a high-school guy —"

"Look, let's *hope* not," Ainslee said, and they both started laughing.

They were laughing so hard that at first they didn't notice the petite older woman come up and stand beside them.

"Girls, I don't believe we've met." Mrs. Whittingham held out a small, bony, fragile-looking hand.

Ainslee covered her mouth and stifled one final giggle. "Hi. I'm Ainslee Smythe."

"And I'm Holly Bannon."

Mrs. Whittingham might have looked dainty, but her grip was strong and impressive as she greeted Holly with a handshake. "Bannon, eh? Yes, I see the resemblance. Your sisters were gems. Absolute gems," Mrs. Whittingham said.

It was the bane of Holly's existence that she had four older sisters, all of whom just had to be accomplished in some way or other. They were a hard act to follow.

"So is Holly," Ainslee said. "She's actually more of a rock, though. A diamond in the rough."

Mrs. Whittingham gave Ainslee a curious smile. "Funny girl. I like you."

"What I was trying to say was, you can depend on her for anything," Ainslee said. "The snack bar place where she's working is going to be in such good shape."

"Club café," Mrs. Whittingham corrected her. "And I'm glad to hear it." She smiled at both of them. "And now, what's your area of expertise?" she asked Ainslee.

"Tennis."

"And are you any good? What a silly question. Of course you're good — we hired you. But exactly how good a player are you?" Mrs. Whittingham asked Ainslee.

Holly smiled at her blunt question. "She's great, actually."

"I play number-two singles, or I did," Ainslee said. "Next season I'll be number one, for sure."

Mrs. Whittingham tapped her on the arm. "I like your attitude, young lady."

"Well, it's half attitude, and half the fact that the number one player graduated," Ainslee admitted.

"Ah! But who cares, as long as it works. Right?" Mrs. Whittingham smiled. "Now, since you're new, do you know everyone here?"

Holly stared right at the guy that she'd spotted from a distance as *the guy I most likely want to succeed in meeting.* "Not yet."

"I could introduce you around," Mrs. Whittingham offered. "Let's see, where shall we start. . . ."

How about right over there? Holly wanted to say. *Right beside the pool, that group of guys we don't know yet, but we would really like to?*

"Excuse me. Mrs. Whittingham?" A woman in a maid's uniform waited politely by her side.

"Yes?"

"Would you like to come inspect the cake before we cut it?" the maid asked.

"No. I'd like to cut it myself," Mrs. Whittingham said. "Make sure it's done properly. Besides, I enjoy a little extra frosting now and then. When you're eighty, you have to look for the small pleasures in life. Excuse me, girls — but don't leave until you have some cake!"

"We won't," Holly promised.

"To summer!" Mrs. Whittingham said,

interrupting Holly's thoughts. The petite owner raised a cup of lemonade.

"To summer!" Holly sipped her lemonade, which still tasted a little strange to her. "Thank you for having us over!" she called as Mrs. Whittingham walked away.

"My pleasure!" Mrs. Whittingham gave a little wave over her shoulder. "It's great to have another Bannon with us!"

"Kiss-up," Ainslee muttered under her breath.

"You're just mad I said something first," Holly replied.

"You're such a . . . Bannon," Ainslee said. "You're très Bannonesque."

Holly pushed Ainslee's arm. "Okay, so. Moving on. Mrs. Whittingham was nice and all, but have you thought of a decent way for us to meet those guys yet?"

Ainslee looked around the party. "We're new here, right? So maybe we don't know where everything is. You could go ask them for directions to the bathroom."

"Are you serious?" Holly wasn't about to embarrass herself like that. "Right. Why don't *you*?" she suggested.

"No, you."

Holly shook her head. "No."

"Okay, then. Grab a tray. Go over and offer them something to eat," Ainslee suggested. "Then introduce yourself. It'll be natural because you can say you're working for the kitchen this summer, and this is part of the job. Go on. Do it."

"Won't that be kind of obvious?" asked Holly.

"Everything's going to feel obvious to *us*, but it won't be to them. They're guys," Ainslee said. "They don't notice anything. And remember — we said we were going to be more bold this summer. So. Go."

"Right. Okay. We did say that." Trying to look casual, Holly ambled over to the tent where the caterers had set up.

"Excuse me," she said to a man wearing the standard black-and-white catering outfit. "Would it be okay if I walked around with a tray of something?"

"A tray of something?" He frowned at her. "Why would you want to do that?"

"Well, see, I'm working in the kitchen this summer — the, uh, club café — and I need the practice," Holly said with a smile.

He stared at her as if she had lost her mind.

"But . . . the club's café doesn't have waited tables."

Did he have to be such a know-it-all? Holly wondered. "I know, I know, but still. It's customer service, right? So it's good practice. Would it be okay?"

"I suppose. I'll have a seat for ten seconds while you do that. Here, I was just about to bring these out. Shrimp puffs. Make the rounds," he said. "But don't let that group over there take them all." He pointed to the group of guys that Holly planned on making a beeline toward.

"No problem. I'll watch them like a hawk." Holly lifted the tray. "Thanks! This will be great."

"Okay, whatever." The caterer sank onto a folding chair, looking spent.

This is like something out of a movie, Holly thought as she approached the group of guys beside the pool. *But it works in the movies, so why not here?*

She assumed as casual an expression as possible while she walked up to them. She took a deep breath to compose herself. *Don't say anything stupid,* she told herself. *Just make eye contact and smile.*

She walked up to the edge of the group and stopped. The guys were joking and laughing about something and didn't notice her at first. *Maybe I should just step away,* she thought as she stared at the back of Extremely Cute Guy's blue T-shirt, which was sort of extremely cute even from the back. *Forget this whole idea.*

Holly cleared her throat. "Excuse me, would you care for a —"

Extremely Cute Guy quickly turned around. The shuffleboard stick he had perched on his shoulder came flying straight at Holly's face.

"Ack!" Holly jumped out of the way — and into the pool, feetfirst.

Somehow, because she landed in the shallow end, she managed to hold the tray upright. "Shrimp puff?" she offered as Extremely Cute Guy stared down at her, his friends gathering behind him.

He didn't jump in to rescue her.

He didn't hold out his hand and pull her toward the edge. He didn't apologize for nearly making her lose an eye.

Instead he just said, "Swim much?" and laughed with his friends. Loudly. At her.

Holly felt like tossing the tray — along with the

12

contents of the pool — back in his face. *Swim much?* What kind of a thing to say was that to a person who nearly drowned — of embarrassment, anyway?

Trying to keep her cool, or what was left of it, Holly set the appetizer tray on the pool deck and climbed out of the pool. She squeezed the hem of her tee and water spilled onto the pool deck. Her shorts were drenched. Her flip-flops were floating in the pool. She crouched down to pick them up, grateful that plastic, or whatever they were made of, floated.

She glanced around for Ainslee, wondering where she'd gone to all of a sudden. What good was a best friend if she didn't run to your rescue when you needed her? And. She. Needed. Rescuing.

Fortunately, the guys had gone back to their game of shuffleboard. All except for one, who was staring at her as she stood up from claiming her flip-flops.

"Hey, you all right?" he asked.

"I'm fine," Holly said. Unless you were bothered by little things like blushing and public humiliation.

"I'm Ross."

"Holly. Hey." She greeted him with a wet wave. "Nice to meet you."

"Nice dive," he said, with a slight nod. "What was that, two and a half somersaults?"

Well, it was one way to meet guys. Maybe not the *best* way, and maybe not the ones you planned on meeting, but still.

"Pike position," Holly replied. "It was difficult, but I've been training for years." Her older sister Maddie had been on the swim team, and she'd picked up a lot of the terms.

"You know diving?" Ross asked, looking impressed. "Sweet."

A maid rushed over and handed Holly a large peach-colored, monogrammed towel. "Please. Be decent!" she said in a disapproving tone.

Wasn't I being decent? Holly wondered. Then she realized: She could be in a wet T-shirt contest. And she didn't want to be. And here she was standing and talking to a guy.

"Excuse me, I'm going to go dry off — see you around," Holly said. She started walking across the lawn and saw Ainslee skipping toward her. "Ains! Where have you *been*?"

"What happened to you? I turned around for, like, two seconds and you're drenched. Let's go

14

inside and find a hair dryer, at least. You are not going to spend the rest of the night looking like *that*," Ainslee declared.

"Thanks." Holly set the tray on the caterer's table as they walked past. "Sorry about the puffs."

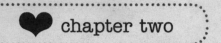

chapter two

"Do you think it's all right if I play wearing this? I mean, I think they said something about wearing tennis whites. But I hardly own any tennis whites, and besides, they make me look sort of washed-out, and I'd rather wear pink." Ainslee was wearing a bright pink mesh polo shirt and a short pale pink tennis skirt, and a pink tennis visor holding back her hair.

"I'm sure it's fine." Holly pulled her long, sandy-brown hair back from behind her ears into a tight ponytail. She hoped she looked okay. If she ran into some of those guys from the party the night before, she wanted to look good. Translation: better than she did in sopping-wet clothes, after making an idiot of herself.

"Do you think shorts and a baby tee fit under the description of 'neat but casual'?" she asked Ainslee.

"In my world, yes. But you're going to look

16

funny if you have to wear an apron. You'll look like you don't have any clothes on." Ainslee laughed.

"Hey, maybe I'll drum up some extra business," Holly joked.

"You mean, business on the side."

"Shut up."

Holly and Ainslee were sitting by the fountain outside the Ridgemont Country Club's entrance. They'd just been dropped off by Holly's mom, who was in charge of driving them to work on Mondays, Wednesdays, and Fridays. Ainslee's dad would drive them to work the other days of the week.

The Ridgemont Athletic Club had been state-of-the-art . . . thirty years ago. Now it was state-of-history. For instance, the fountain they were sitting in front of had about four spouts that didn't work, making the whole display off-center. The fountain randomly misfired water, occasionally drenching people who sat too close to it, or at the exact wrong angle. Holly had found that out the hard way, when she had showed up early for her interview and sat in just the wrong spot. Fortunately, she only got a wet sleeve.

"If only the club was as nice as Mrs.

Whittingham's house," Ainslee mused. "Would you call that a house or a mansion?"

"I'd call it time to remodel this place. Do you think our phones will even work in there?" Holly took out her cell phone and glanced at the time. "And why are we always early for everything?"

"I don't know, but it's definitely a character flaw. On the plus side, it gives us a chance to check out other people showing up," Ainslee said. "So it was worth getting up early for that."

"I can't believe my name tag is spelled wrong. Holli. Who has the name Holli? I've never even seen it before." She twirled the red plastic tag in her fingers.

"At least you got one. They didn't even have anything close to my name. Which is fine, because who needs a name tag poking through their shirt? It would ruin my look, anyway. They must be trying to use old name tags," Ainslee said. "Reuse, recycle, and all that. You know what? You could add 'ster' to the end. Hollister. Maybe go by a different name this summer."

"Hollister Bannon. I like it. Except I sound like a guy," Holly complained.

"And a clothes store," Ainslee pointed out.

"Maybe I just won't wear the name tag until

I can fix it," Holly said. "Or, ever. Name tags are so . . ."

"Tacky. Ugly. Pointless," Ainslee suggested.

"Exactly. So let's not wear them," Holly suggested. "Let's start a trend. People either remember our names, or they don't."

They both watched a Jeep's tires squeal as it came to a stop in the parking lot. Four guys hopped out and headed toward the club.

"Speaking of not knowing names. Have you ever seen them before? Now this is what I'm talking about. Très sweet." Ainslee had just finished her second year of French class and, in Holly's opinion, was getting a little carried away with practicing it. "You know what? They're college guys," Ainslee murmured as she watched them. "Too old."

"How can you tell?" Holly asked.

"I just can," Ainslee said.

"It's your gift," Holly teased her.

"Sure. One of the many." Ainslee gestured to a guy walking in from the parking lot. "That's Ross White. Remember him? He's on the tennis team at school."

"He's the guy who helped me out of the pool last night!" Holly said. "He was really nice."

"He would be cooler if he didn't wear a head-band when he plays. He thinks he's Roger Federer," Ainslee said under her breath. "Hey, Ross. How's it going?" she called to him.

"Ainslee! Want to warm up?" he called back. His thick blond hair was shoulder length and flopped in his eyes. He was carrying a bag of tennis rackets.

"I'll be there in a sec," Ainslee promised.

"Cool." He pushed his hair back from his forehead as he strode past.

"You know, maybe he wears the headband not because of Roger, but because he gets hot under all that floppy hair," Holly commented quietly. "So does that make him not fling material? The headband?"

Ainslee tapped her finger against her chin. "I'm not sure yet. I mean, I'm all for making personal fashion statements when you're on the court. Like Serena Williams."

"Your idol," Holly said.

"Exactly. But it just seems kind of more cool when it's a girl doing it, you know? Anyway. I suppose he could be perfect, because summer's different. Summer you don't want anything serious or long-lasting, because you'll probably go separate ways when school starts."

"You definitely read that out of a magazine," Holly said.

"But a fling this summer, you have to admit, would be nice," Ainslee commented. "Just picture it. No strings attached. Just something semi-romantic and fun, and someone to pine over when you go back to school and everyone asks how your summer was, and you have this amazing story about a lifeguard —"

"Or not," Holly interjected. "Because the lifeguards here are Kate Tucker and Angela Lane, aren't they?"

Ainslee waved her hand in the air. "Whatever. That was just an example. Anyway, *speaking* of romantic flings," she said.

"What?" Holly said.

"And flings into the pool," Ainslee added. "Or I guess technically it was a leap, wasn't it?"

"Oh, no. Are you trying to say —"

"Blue T-shirt guy coming this way."

"That's what I thought you meant." Holly figured it was probably too late to run off and hide, so she crouched down a bit behind the pathetically gurgling fountain and watched him walk toward the building. Maybe he'd be too distracted by the fact that the automatic entrance doors were actually working for once to notice that she was sitting right there.

He wore slouchy khaki shorts and a club T-shirt, and for some reason they looked better on him than they did on anyone else. If there were a Ridgemont Country Club catalog? He'd be the model on the cover. In fact, he sort of reminded her of a guy in the latest J. Crew catalog. The one her parents had told her to recycle, because they weren't about to pay for anything in it, which was when she'd decided to definitely get a summer job.

Ainslee peered around the fountain at Holly. "Are you trying to be invisible? Because you're not. You don't have that superpower."

"Shut up," Holly whispered, as he neared them.

"Hey! How's it going?" Ainslee said as he got closer.

Holly wanted to shove her into the fountain's pool. Wasn't the whole point *not* to attract attention to themselves?

"What's up?" he replied, briefly nodding at

both of them as he went past and into the building.

"Did you notice that he's still cute in the day-light?" Ainslee asked.

"Yeah, I did. Thanks for mentioning that," Holly said. "You know, I could kill you now, but that would ruin your summer fling prospects," she muttered.

"Hey. My mom says that if you like someone, you have to let him know," Ainslee said. "So next time you see him, make sure you say hi."

"Right."

"It's hi. It's not I love you or anything," Ainslee said. "It's a fling. That's all."

"A fling," Holly murmured. Well, he was definitely someone she wanted to find out more about. But then she remembered his comment the night before. *Swim much?* Maybe she should refocus her attention on someone else — someone a little less *rude*.

Oh, well. At least she had a job at the club, which was the only cool place in town to work. Cool . . . unless you got the one position that involved cooking and grilling. It wasn't that it would be a bad job at all — it just had the potential to be hot.

It was her fault for filling out her application late, and for not having any real skill except cooking, which she'd highlighted in her application because the rest of it looked so, uh, blank.

"Oops — it's ten o'clock, we'd better go." Ainslee got to her feet and lifted her duffel bag. "So. See you at three, right? For your so-called lesson?"

"Translation: hanging out with you? Right. Good luck!" Holly called to Ainslee as they split up. She walked through the main building, past the membership office, the racquetball courts, and the locker room entrances.

She stopped outside the kitchen's back door and stood in the doorway for a second. There was a guy standing over by the giant stainless refrigerator.

He closed the door and turned around.

Him! she thought.

Oh, no. Not him.

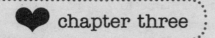

chapter three

"Hey. Who are you?" he said.

It wasn't exactly the politest greeting in history.

"Hi," she said. "Holly Bannon." She wanted to look at him, but she also wanted to run and hide. When was he going to recognize her from the night before and her disastrous plunge with shrimp puffs?

Stop pounding, stop pounding, stop pounding, she tried to tell her pulse, which was beating like a loud bass drum.

"Hey. I'm Paul West," he introduced himself.

And then she remembered why he looked so familiar. Of course. Paul West. Soccer star. Who went to Southwest High School. Who had headlines about him in the newspaper like "Go (South)West, Young Man," and "West by Southwest."

She unclipped her name tag and grabbed a

pen from the jar on the counter. Holly started changing the *i* in her name to a *y*, but it was hard to do because the tag was plastic and the ink smudged, so now her name looked like "Hollw-something."

"It's supposed to say Holly," she explained.

"Oh. I saw the last name Bannon over here, on the staff list. I thought it was your sister. See, it says B. Bannon." He showed her the list, pointing to the spot where her name appeared — or didn't.

"You're kidding — they got that wrong, too? It should be an *H*. Not a *B*." Holly gave up on her name tag and turned to look at him.

"An *H*?" he asked.

"If you're disappointed, that's okay, most people are," Holly said.

"What? What are you talking about? I'm not," he said. "That wasn't what I was thinking at all."

"Really?" she asked, finding that hard to believe. His face had definitely fallen when he saw it was her and not Bethany. Or at least changed, anyway.

"You don't know what I'm thinking."

"Probably not." *Hopefully not something like: Gosh, you sure don't look anything like your drop-*

dead-gorgeous older sister. She laughed nervously. "Sorry, I just get that a lot."

"No problem. Your sister did work at the club last summer, right?" he asked.

Holly nodded. "Bethany. Right. She worked in the membership office."

"Okay, that's it. I hardly ever saw her, though. She never came to any of the employee parties." He took a sip from a can of orange juice. "She was kind of standoffish, actually."

Did you ever think that maybe it was you? Holly wondered. Say what you wanted about Bethany — she did seem to have good taste when it came to guys.

"You think so? That's funny. She's usually goes to parties, but sometimes she gets invited to more than one, so . . ." Holly said. No, that wouldn't do it — that would only intrigue him more. She coughed. "Actually, what it was, was that she and her boyfriend spent all their time together last summer. Like. *All* their time."

"Huh. Whatever." He didn't seem heartbroken, which was good. He shrugged, then went back to sorting the ketchup and mustard packets into a plastic container.

Holly looked around the kitchen. It was a little dated, like everything else in the club — the appliances looked about a hundred years old. Some of them were actually *avocado*-colored.

There was a counter with a canvas tarp hanging down to cover the window, because they weren't open for business yet. The dining area was outside on a patio, not far from the outdoor pool. Already, Holly could hear little kids laughing and shouting as they played in the water.

She tried to think of something else to say. "So, uh, how long have you worked here?" she asked.

"This will be my second summer." Paul opened a box of relish packets and filled a plastic container that stacked on top of the ketchup and mustard.

"Really? That's cool. And, uh, where do you go to school?" she asked. She knew already, but she wasn't about to let on that she knew, because that would make her seem like a groupie or something. When she wasn't — the reason she knew about him and soccer was that she was on her school team, too.

She was waiting for him to make the connection, to look at her and realize that she was the one who'd leaped into the pool the night before. But it hadn't seemed to register yet. Maybe he'd never remember. Maybe it had been too dark for him to see what she really looked like. She could start all over and make a not-so-horrible impression this time.

"I go to Southwest," he said as he arranged the containers on the counter. "You?"

"East," she said.

"Huh," he commented.

And then there was this very awkward, very quiet pause. Holly looked around for a radio to turn on, or a blender, or something. She was starting to feel really stupid, just standing there watching him work.

"So, anyway, Bethany's off on a . . . tour this summer," she explained. "With SFABT."

Paul gave her a confused look. "With what? Or did you just sneeze?"

"No, sorry," Holly laughed. "SFABT. It stands for Students for a Better Tomorrow."

"Oh." Paul looked surprised. "Really? She does that?"

"Does what?"

"That kind of, uh . . . happy singing thing?"

Holly laughed. "Yeah."

"That's weird. When I saw her around here last summer, I always thought she was normal."

"She *is* normal." *At least, most of the time,* Holly thought. "This is my sister you're insulting." She felt like she needed to stand up for Bethany, but he had a point. Singing about positivity every single day had to get old, didn't it? Still, if her angelic and beautiful sister wanted to hit the road for the summer, that was her right. The song "Just Say No to a No Attitude" was a bit over the top, though.

"Sorry, I didn't mean it like that. Sure, she's, like, totally normal." He smiled at her. "In a really . . . happy kind of a way. Does that run in the family?"

"No! I don't sing," Holly said.

"I meant the happiness part."

"Oh, yeah. Definitely." Holly smiled. *At least, happy to be here. With you. I think.*

He looked at her for another second, and she noticed his eyes were brown with little black flecks in them.

She didn't know what to say. She patted the stainless exterior of the ice machine. "Nice ice machine," she mumbled. "It's so clean." *So very, very clean. And I sound so very, very stupid.*

"Yeah, and it works pretty well, most of the time. Did Russell give you the tour yesterday? Did he go over stuff with you and train you?" Paul asked.

Holly nodded. She'd spent about two hours learning everything there was to know about the kitchen, the grill, storage, cooking, and the refrigerator. It wasn't all that complicated.

The club café served muffins, sandwiches, burgers, a few salads, and frozen ice-cream "novelties," like Fudgsicles and Popsicles. Customers came to a walk-up window, placed their order, then sat at tables until their name was called. The tables were outside on a patio, with large umbrellas to protect customers from the sun and rain. Not too far off in the distance was the club's outdoor pool, and just past that was the eighteen-hole golf course. The tennis courts, where Ainslee worked, were on the other side of the club, entirely out of view.

"Okay, so did Russell tell you about the soda machine? How you put the syrup in?" Paul asked.

She nodded. "And he told me about the lemonade, the iced tea, the combination lemonade and iced tea, which is called an Arnold Schwarzenegger —"

"Arnold *Palmer*," Paul corrected. "Palmer. Famous golf player."

"That's it. Right. Does Tiger Woods have his own beverage yet?"

Paul just rolled his eyes.

"Not funny. Okay. Russell also showed me what he calls the binder for dummies, which has all the info I'll need. Like, how to make a cheese sandwich. It's kind of insulting, but I'll get over it."

"Yeah, well, no offense, but we've had dummies here before," Paul said, "which is why he made it. So the menu's right there." Paul pointed to the wall. The menu was the kind with a white ridged background, where you posted up black letters and numbers for the prices.

GRILLED CHEESE

GRILLED CHEESE WITH TOMATO

CHEESEBURGER

A few of the letters had fallen off, so there were odd listings like:

IC D TEA

HA BURGER

ALL-BEE HOT DOG

"What's an all-bee hot dog? Sounds danger-
ous," Holly joked. "Does that come with one of
those antiallergy shots on the side?"

Paul didn't laugh. "It stands for beef. Obviously.
We're missing some letters."

Holly wondered if that was because they'd had
the same menu board since 1980. "Huh. So, what
do, uh, people order the most?" Holly asked, desperate to make conversation, to say anything that
would make him *not* remember what a klutz she'd
been last night.

"It depends how old they are. The old people
order club sandwiches. The little kids order grilled
cheese. Everyone in the middle has burgers," he
replied.

"So you've figured this out. You did a study?"
Holly teased.

He turned and gave her an unfriendly glare.
"It's just something you learn when you've been
here a while." He sprayed the counter and wiped
it clean.

He had a bit of an attitude, but she decided to
give him the benefit of the doubt.

"Well, maybe it's too easy. Maybe it means we

need more stuff on the menu or something." Holly laughed nervously.

"There's nothing *wrong* with the menu," Paul said. "Nobody complains about it, ever."

"Right. Okay." Holly couldn't believe he was being conceited about a silly menu. And was knowing what people wanted to order that amazing, really? The menu was only ten lines long.

"Are you sure you know everything?" Paul asked. "Because we're going to open soon and I'm not sure you're ready."

Holly raised one eyebrow. "Why don't you go over things for me?" she said, as politely as she could manage it.

He dropped the cleaning products as if he'd just been dying for a chance to show her how much he knew. "Okay. So, this is where you clock in and write down your hours. This is the pantry. The deep-freeze. We order food twice a week, but usually Russell does that."

Holly nodded politely. She knew all this from her meeting with Russell, but if going over it all again made Paul happy — or at least less rude — she didn't mind. She wouldn't want to mess up on her first day, and besides, she didn't mind listening to his voice.

34

"This is where you keep your soda cup," Paul explained, pointing to a small shelf beside the refrigerator. "Water bottle, whatever. Put your initials on it."

"Okay, but . . . how many other people work here?" asked Holly.

Paul shrugged. "Just us. Well, except Russell, when he fills in for us."

"So . . . won't we know which bottle is ours? It would be either yours or mine?"

He glared at her for a second. "It makes things easier, okay? Trust me. I worked here last summer."

Which he'd already mentioned more than once. So, he was an expert in both bottle possession and order prediction. "Right. Okay," Holly said. He might be slightly good-looking, but why was he acting like her boss? He was her coworker.

She'd had enough of being bossed around by her older sisters — who were now, thankfully, off at college, holding down jobs, or touring around the world in bizarre singing acts. Sometimes that made their big house seem lonely, but sometimes it was pure heaven to have the place mostly to herself.

"I guess we should get started," Holly said. "What should I do first? I think Russell said something about prepping for lunch. Does lunch really start at ten-thirty?"

"Some people come by after early morning golf or tennis, but the real rush starts around eleven. I'm going to heat the grill. If you want, I guess you can chop the lettuce and slice the tomatoes." He said it like he was doing her a favor, when it sounded to Holly like she'd be doing a lot more work than he would.

"Great!" Holly said. She washed her hands in the sink, then pulled the vegetables out of the large, oversize refrigerator and set them on the counter. She pulled a knife off the magnetic rack by the sink and, after washing the lettuce and tomatoes, started to chop and slice.

Paul came to stand beside her for a second. She noticed that he was about half a foot taller than she was, which meant he was about six feet. *Perfect*, she thought. Well, if height was all that mattered.

"Is that hard work for you?" he asked.

"No, not really." Holly felt herself start to blush. "We always have these big family parties where we fix all the food, so I'm used to being put on chopping detail."

"Huh. Well, it's just that you look sort of red, like you're working really hard at that," Paul commented. "It's not that difficult."

Holly grit her teeth to keep from punching him in the gut. She was holding a knife and that probably wouldn't end well. "No, it's not hard at all," she replied with a cheerful smile. What was he getting at?

"You look hot," he said.

Thanks, Holly thought. *So do you. Too bad you're so . . . bossy.* She focused on slicing the tomatoes again. "I think maybe it's just from standing beside the grill," she said.

"I just turned it on. It's not hot yet," he said, staring at her.

"You know what? Maybe we could open another window." She leaned over the grill toward a small window at that end of the kitchen. Suddenly there was a whooshing sound and one of the gas flames flared out from underneath the grill surface, nearly singeing her arm. "Yikes!"

"Sorry. I forgot to tell you about that," he said.

Funny, he'd told her everything *but* that, Holly thought. "You forgot to tell me?" she cried. "Forgot? Or deliberately left out the fact I was about to go up in flames?"

"Don't overreact or anything. I was *going* to tell you when we got to the grill training part," Paul said. "You have to look out for that burner. It flares up at random moments."

"Yeah, well. Thanks for the warning. Safety first," Holly muttered. Wasn't that what Russell had said? She went back to chopping, while Paul worked on getting out dishes and silverware. She peeked over at him out of the corner of her eye. Was he as much of a jerk as he seemed, or were they just getting off on the wrong foot? Did he think he owned the place or something?

Wait. Did he? What if he were related to Mrs. Whittingham? She was sunk, if that was the case.

Funny how this was his second summer. What had happened to his last coworker? Obviously he or she hadn't come back.

She turned to rinse a speck of dirt off some lettuce leaves. Paul turned around with a tray and she veered out of the way, nearly putting her hands on the grill.

"Watch it!" he cried.

"It's not *me*!" Holly replied, thinking the kitchen was a little small for two people who didn't get along all that well yet. "Why are you looking at me like that?"

"Because. I just realized something," Paul said, with a smile. "That was you last night!"

"Me? What do you, ah, mean, that was me?" she asked casually.

"That so was you. You fell into the pool at Mrs. Whittingham's." Paul looked excited by the fact that he'd just realized it.

Holly continued to chop away, pretending this didn't bother her. "I didn't fall. Exactly. I jumped — to get out of the way of *you*," she said.

Paul tossed a couple of mangled straws into the trash can. "That was so funny."

"Yeah. Hilarious. Thanks for caring." Holly glared at him.

"What? Why are you looking at me like that?" Paul held up his hands. "I didn't do anything."

"You practically pushed me into the pool, like I was a shuffleboard plate!" Holly said.

"Plate?" He started to laugh. "Like this?" He picked up a paper plate and waved it in front of her face.

She wasn't going to tell him that the breeze felt

good. "Whatever you call those shuffleboard thingies."

"Discs."

"Do I look like I play shuffleboard?" Holly snapped.

"Sorry. I didn't realize you were so sensitive."

Holly decided to ignore that last comment and get to work, waiting on their first customer.

"It's okay, I'll get it." He pushed past her to the counter.

The lack of space in the kitchen is definitely going to be a problem, Holly thought.

"Club sandwich, extra tomatoes," the older man said. "I'd like some mustard on there as well."

"I'll have that right up for you. Condiments are on the counter, sir," Paul said. He turned to Holly. "See, told you the old folks ordered the club," he whispered.

"Brilliant," Holly muttered. "Your powers of observation are amazing."

"Just make the toast," he said.

"Fine." Holly grabbed three slices of bread and dropped them into the big toaster. She waited until they popped up, then lifted them out with tongs and put them on a paper plate for Paul, who was standing beside her, cold cuts at the ready.

"Well, that's not right," he said, frowning at the bread.

"How can that be wrong? It's toast," Holly said.

"It's done too much," he complained.

"I think it's fine. It's lightly browned. That's how Russell told me it should be. I didn't even change the little dial thingy!"

"I guess it's okay. But I'll adjust the dials for next time."

Oh, no. I'm working with a toast freak, Holly thought.

The next few orders didn't go any more smoothly. Whatever Holly attempted, Paul corrected her. The way she grilled the hamburger buns was wrong. The way she melted the cheese on top of the burgers was wrong. Even the way she filled a cup halfway with ice was wrong.

"That's the way Russell showed me," Holly said. "Half a cup of ice."

"Well, it's wrong. It's one-third ice, two-thirds soda. I mean, obviously."

Obviously nothing, she was thinking. And obviously? She and Paul weren't exactly hitting it off.

"You know, all you need is a little experience and you'll do fine." He patted her shoulder as she brought the soda to a waiting customer.

She gazed out at the pool for a second, wishing she was there instead of here. Then she smiled as a group of guys carrying golf club bags approached the counter. Forget Paul. She could meet plenty of other guys at this job. Ones that didn't mock her every move.

At least, she hoped so.

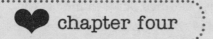

chapter four

At three o'clock, Holly ran off to meet Ainslee at the tennis courts. She couldn't wait to tell her that so far the first day had gone both horribly and also terribly.

She needed to give Ainslee all the painful details about Paul. Immediately. Then she could begin purging them from her brain.

Except maybe the detail where she'd gotten to stand right next to him at the counter and their elbows had been almost touching for almost thirty seconds. Which would have been exciting, if he hadn't then told her that they were running short on dishes and she should go wash some. And then proceed to give her a lesson on how much dish detergent to use in ratio to dishes.

Wow. He looked cute, but the attraction ended there. A fling was totally out of the question. She didn't want to spend any more time with Paul than she absolutely had to.

Holly walked into the Racquet Club Center —
which was actually a glorified office in the hallway
closest to the tennis courts, with a large picture
window that looked out on the four courts. There
were posters on the wall of various tennis players,
but most of them were players Holly had never
heard of who held strange, small rackets.

"Ains?" she called as she walked in.

But Ainslee wasn't there. Instead, around the
corner from the door, Ross of the floppy blond
hair was sitting back in a chair, with his feet up
on the desk. He was sipping a Red Bull and he
looked as relaxed as any human being could be.
Something about him reminded her of the actor
Owen Wilson.

"Hi," Holly said. "I'm here for my lesson. Is
Ainslee around?"

"Nope. Ainslee's busy," Ross said. He took a
drink from the can. "Someone needed a fourth."

"A fourth what?" asked Holly.

"Player for mixed doubles. And I mean, if
you're going to choose a player, you can't do any
better than Ainslee."

"True," Holly agreed.

"Don't worry, I'll take care of you," Ross
promised. He smiled at her.

He would "take care" of her? *Why?* she wondered. And was that a good thing?

"No, but see, I'm here for my lesson. With Ainslee," Holly insisted. She peered out at the courts. Where *was* she? Couldn't the game be over by now? And if they needed a fourth, wasn't someone else around?

Then she saw a pink blur as a player rushed to the net to hit an overhead smash. Ainslee pumped her fist in the air, like she was enjoying herself.

"Isn't she great?" Ross asked.

"Sure. Yes," Holly said. *She's great, except for the fact that she's stranding me for my tennis lesson.* And Holly really needed to talk to her. "Okay, so I should come back later. What time is good?"

"She's booked all afternoon, so I rescheduled you. I'll be giving your lesson." Ross drained the rest of the energy drink and crumpled the can in his fist, then tossed it into a recycling bin by the doorway.

"You?" Holly asked. She wasn't good enough to take a lesson from a guy on the varsity tennis team. She'd rather die, or go back to work.

"Sure, me. Why not? It'll be fun." He glanced at the clipboard on his desk, then smiled at her. "Hey, you know what, you look familiar."

"We talked last night. By the pool?" Holly said.

"Oh, yeah. Right." Ross nodded, as if he was only just now remembering. He seemed a little on the spacey side. "But I meant, before then."

"We go to the same school," Holly told him.

"Really? Huh. But we don't have any classes together, do we?"

"No. But maybe you knew one of my older sisters. Bethany? Arianna?"

Ross shook his head. "No. It's not that."

"Plus I hang out with Ainslee all the time," Holly said, as if that wasn't totally obvious. Maybe he'd been hit on the head a few times during a tennis match. "And since you guys are both on the tennis team together . . . Well, anyway. I guess it's not important." *Except that the longer I keep talking, the less time I'll have to be on the tennis court with you.*

No offense. I just don't exactly play all that well, and I'd rather have a lesson with Roger Federer or Andy Roddick, because at least afterward they wouldn't go back to my school and tell everyone how horrible and uncoordinated I was.

"That must be it," Ross said. "Whenever I see Ainslee, you guys are usually hanging out." He nodded. "So, Holly. You want to get started?" Ross smiled at her.

"Okay . . . I guess." Holly didn't have a good feeling about this. The only reason she'd signed up for tennis lessons at all was to hang out with Ainslee, and to get her parents off her back. They insisted she take advantage of the club's offer of discounted classes and do something athletic this summer. Never mind that she played soccer and was running three days a week to get in shape for the fall season.

She followed Ross outside, and they walked to the first court, the one nearest the building. It was the farthest from the one where Ainslee was playing.

"Don't worry, Ainslee. I'll take care of it!" Ross called to her, just as she was about to serve.

She cast him an annoyed glance. "Great!" she called back with a phony smile, then she waved at Holly before resuming her match.

Holly didn't know much about tennis, or the players who played it. She'd watched some of Ainslee's matches, and that was about it. She wasn't exactly a natural.

Ross wheeled a metal basket of tennis balls

onto the middle of the court. Did he really expect her to hit all of those?

"You know I'm, uh, a beginner, right?" Holly said.

"We'll see. I want you to hit a few before I evaluate where you are. Give it your best shot!" Ross called over the net.

Did he really just say that? Holly groaned. A tennis pun?

She was supposed to be taking it easy this hour, not going to tennis camp. "It's just, um, do we need that many tennis balls?" she asked.

"Yup. We're going to be moving nonstop for the next hour." Ross bounced up and down on his sneakers, tapping the palm of one hand against his racket strings. He looked like he was preparing to return a serve. From Roger Federer. "Okay, are you ready? Let's start with some forehands."

Forehands. Holly looked at the way Ross was turned. She swiveled and prepared to hit the ball Ross was launching over the net.

She tried swinging at the ball, but it sailed right past her.

The next one bounced right in front of her. She missed that one, too.

"Nice shot!" she heard someone shout.

She looked around to see who was making fun of her, but apparently the voice had come from a nearby court. When she looked back at Ross, another ball was sailing right past her.

"Sorry!" she called to him.

"Hey, it's okay!" Ross called across the net. "Don't sweat it."

Holly kept trying, and finally connected with a few balls, but it seemed as if every shot she made either went long or into the net.

"Good work! You know, all you need is a little more experience," said Ross as they met at the net.

"I really, really wish people would stop saying that." Holly sighed.

His eyebrows shot up, as if no one had ever spoken rudely to him before.

"Sorry," Holly apologized, wiping her forehead with a small towel. "I just hate it when I can't do something."

"You'll get the hang of it. Don't give up — we've still got half an hour." He grinned at her, as if this were a good thing.

Holly nearly dropped her racket.

When the club café closed for the day, Holly couldn't believe how tired she felt. They hadn't even been that busy. *Maybe it was the tennis lesson, then,* she thought. *And the fact that Ross is training me for Wimbledon.*

Ainslee's eyes widened as she walked up to Holly and Paul, who were locking the kitchen door for the night.

"So, are you guys as beat as I am? And hot? There is air-conditioning in the kitchen, right?" Ainslee asked.

"Yeah, we just can't feel it most of the time," Paul answered.

"I was thinking we should go for a swim before we head home. I called my mom and she said that was okay — she'll come by in an hour to get us," she said to Holly.

"Sounds good." Holly stood there for a second before realizing Paul and Ainslee had never met. "Paul, this is Ainslee," Holly said.

"Hey." Paul nodded. "What do you do here?"

"Tennis," Ainslee said.

"You're a club pro?" Paul asked. "Cool."

"Well, I'm not *exactly* a club pro," Ainslee admitted. "I mean you have to be licensed for that, I think."

"So you're semipro," Holly said.

Ainslee smiled. "Exactly."

"Huh. Does that count for anything?" Paul asked.

Ainslee stared at him. "Excuse me?"

"I mean, couldn't anyone show up and call themselves a semipro?" he said.

"Why don't you try it and find out?" Ainslee replied. "I'm pretty sure I could beat you. In fact, Mrs. Whittingham could probably beat you."

Holly laughed. "Ouch."

"How do you know? You've never seen me play," Paul grumbled.

"Exactly." Ainslee folded her arms and smiled at him. "Anyway. You want to go swimming with us or not?" she asked Paul, undeterred by his know-it-all attitude.

"Pool privileges are a definite perk of the job," he agreed. "I don't know. Maybe I'll see you there." He jogged away down the hall.

"Can you believe I'm working with him?" Holly asked. "With him. *The* guy. More like, can you believe how rude he is?"

"No, I can't believe it. But the question is, did you meet anyone *else* today so far?" Ainslee asked. "Besides rude guy?"

51

"He's not that rude," Holly said. "Well, maybe he is. I did talk to this one other guy, but he was too old. Like a college junior."

"Hmm. Well, I had to play against a sixty-eight-year-old," Ainslee said. "If you want to talk about *old*."

Holly laughed as they walked into the women's locker room to change into their suits. Once inside a dressing room, Holly pulled her tiny blue bikini out of her duffel bag. She thought about the fact that the pool was probably full of people. She thought about the fact that one of them might be Paul.

"Maybe I shouldn't have packed this suit," Holly said.

"Why not?" Ainslee asked from the dressing room next door. "It looks cool on you. It's your exact eye color."

"Yeah, but . . ." Holly couldn't help wishing that the suit weren't so revealing.

"But nothing. Just keep telling yourself. This is the summer for us," Ainslee said.

"Maybe," Holly said, wishing it were true as she donned the bikini and then undid her hair from its tight ponytail. She brushed her hair and let it fan over her shoulders, giving them a little extra coverage.

"You know, you're turning sixteen in a couple weeks, which is lucky," Ainslee declared as she stepped out wearing a striped bikini. Her long blond hair was tied in a neat French braid.

"It is? I thought it was sweet sixteen. Not lucky sixteen."

"It's both. The only problem is, you're not supposed to date guys you work with," Ainslee said.

"Right, but we'll only be working with them for nine weeks. It's not like an office job where you're there day after day," Holly pointed out.

"True. My mom went out with that guy from her office, remember?" Ainslee said as she leaned close to the mirror and brushed on some pink lip gloss. She groaned. "Quelle disaster that was."

"Okay, I am *not* getting any more love-life advice from your mom," Holly said. "Is that clear?" She wrapped a large club towel strategically around her waist.

They stood in the doorway for a second, looking out at the pool.

"Is that Ross? Swimming laps?" Holly asked.

"He's weird," Ainslee said.

"Why is that weird?"

"Because everyone else is goofing around and having fun, and he's off in lane one, practicing his flip turns."

"Maybe he's on the swim team. Is he?" Holly asked.

"I guess maybe he mentioned that. Which means he could be wearing a Spee —"

"Don't say it." Holly looked back out at Ross. "No, he's not. He's got shorts on. So give him a break."

"Come on, let's go — there's Paul!"

Ainslee pushed Holly in front of her, and they stumbled out onto the pool deck. Holly's foot caught on her towel and pulled it off.

She tried to yank it back up around her waist, but slowly realized someone was holding on to the other end.

"Hey," she said to Paul, who was treading water at the side of the pool, her towel in his hand. "You mind giving that back?"

Paul looked at his friend Toby, who was in the water beside him, his elbows propped on the edge. "What do you think? Five bucks?"

"Are you serious?" Holly tried to ignore the fact that she felt practically naked standing there in front of them. "You're holding my towel hostage?" She tugged at it again. "Come on."

"Dude. Give it back," Toby said.

Ainslee lowered her sunglasses and frowned at him. "If you forgot your own towel, you can get one from the pool desk. Like, how about *now*." She set her sunglasses on a table along with her towel, and quickly headed down the steps into the pool.

"Okay. Sorry," Paul said. "I guess that is kind of dumb. Here." He held up the towel to Holly. "Uh-oh. Don't look now, but . . ." he warned.

"What?"

"Russell." Paul gestured with his chin. "Behind you. And you're not going to believe what he's wearing."

Holly glanced over her shoulder. As she did, Paul pulled the towel, and she toppled and fell into the pool with a loud, awkward splash.

"Got you!" he cried, and he and Toby exchanged high fives.

Holly could have killed him as she grabbed her soggy towel and tossed it up onto the deck.

Maybe she would. Tomorrow. There could be an "accident" involving the grill, or —

"You okay?" Ainslee asked, interrupting her

daydream by swimming over to her. She brushed some water from her eyes.

"Oh, yeah. I'm great," Holly said. "He nearly drowned me!"

Ainslee grinned. "That means he likes you. My mom said —"

Holly sank underwater, letting her hair drift up to the surface. She didn't want to hear any more advice from Ainslee — or Ainslee's mom.

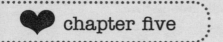

chapter five

Holly leaped to her feet as a customer approached the counter the next morning. She'd decided the night before that she was going to do things differently today. She wasn't going to sit back and watch Paul for another second — that would only make him think he was even *more* important.

"What are you doing?" Paul asked, coming out of the back room.

"Customer. I'll handle —"

"I'll get it," Paul interrupted, rushing up and stepping in front of her. "Sir, the usual?"

Holly watched as Paul rang up the order, washed his hands, and started grilling a hot dog.

How hard was that? Did he really think she couldn't handle that? Of course, there was the overdone toast incident. He might not be able to let that go.

Toast freak.

"You know, eventually you have to let me

actually wait on people," Holly said. "Things could go a lot faster around here."

"What?"

"You keep pushing me out of the way. Kind of like you did yesterday at the pool, when you pushed me in," Holly reminded him.

"Technically I think I actually *pulled* you in," Paul said.

Holly shook her head. "Whatever. It was still uncalled for. And you don't have to do everything here by yourself —"

"But you're new," he said. "And yesterday wasn't that busy so you didn't get to practice —"

"Yeah, and if I never wait on anyone, I'll always be new," Holly said. "So far all I've done is chop stuff and make toast."

"Good point. I just thought, you know, you might want to watch me."

Holly raised one eyebrow and looked at him. Yes, he was good-looking, but he was also obnoxiously conceited. Did he think he was doing brain surgery, or grilling a precooked meat thingy?

"Holly?" He waved the grill tongs in front of her face. "You can take over *now,* if you want."

"No, that's okay. I'll watch," she said. "Probably

still a lot for me to learn from you." *Oh Talented Super Grillmaster*, she wanted to add, but didn't.

"Well, that's true. You don't want to burn the hot dog, but you do want to give it that nice grilled flavor," Paul explained.

It's a hot dog, Holly wanted to say. *Not a steak.*

"Tell you what. Next customer is yours," he promised her.

"Great. Can't wait," she replied.

About five minutes later, a guy wearing a Ridgemont C.C. T-shirt came up to the window. *Does he work here, too?* Holly wondered. He looked like he might work in the weight room. Several hundreds of hours a week.

"Go ahead," Paul urged her, giving her a little nudge with his elbow.

Holly brushed him off as she walked up to the counter. "Hi there. What can I get you?" she asked.

"A large root beer," he said.

"And?" Holly prompted.

He shrugged. "That's it."

"Oh. Okay." She rang up the sale, then grabbed a large paper cup and held it under the ice dispenser. Something in the dispenser malfunctioned and ice cubes spewed everywhere, overfilling the cup, spilling onto her hands, and dropping onto the floor.

"You have to look out for that thing," Paul said. "Press it for more than two seconds and it goes crazy."

"*Now* you tell me," Holly muttered under her breath.

"Sure you don't need to observe just one more day?" Paul teased.

"I'm fine." She dumped most of the massive amounts of ice and filled the cup with root beer. Then she slid it and a straw across the counter. "Here you go!"

"Thanks." The guy smiled at her. He looked like one of the college guys she and Ainslee had checked out a few days ago. He was really good-looking, but he was also probably too old for her.

"Hey, did you work here last summer?" he suddenly asked.

Holly shook her head.

"Yeah, I didn't think I'd seen you before. Cool." He smiled again. "What's your name?"

"Holly."

"Well, see you around, Holly." He tapped the

straw end on the counter to punch it through the wrapper. "Thanks!"

She smiled and waved good-bye, then leaned against the counter and watched him walk away.

Paul tapped her on the shoulder. "You know, you shouldn't talk to customers that long."

"What? You talk to your friends for, like, five minutes!" Holly argued.

"I do not."

"Do too," Holly said.

"Anyway. Regardless. We have work to do," Paul said.

"Oh. We do? Right. Of course we do. Like, uh, what?"

"Slice tomatoes, chop lettuce, get our assembly line going. Lunch rush is coming," Paul said, like it should have been obvious to her that this was a national crisis. "We have to be ready."

Sir, yes sir, Holly wanted to say. He was sort of a perfectionist, which she might admire, if he weren't so annoyingly conceited about being right all the time — and if he didn't constantly tell her what to do.

They worked side by side for a few minutes in silence. Finally Paul asked, "So. What do you do at East?"

"What do I do?" Holly said. What was he getting at? "Take classes?"

Paul rolled his eyes. "*Besides* that."

"Oh. Well, I'm on the events committee, the activity planning committee —"

"Aren't they the same thing?" Paul laughed.

"No, not at all," Holly said. Although, come to think of it, they sort of *were*, except she'd never admit that to Paul. "And I'm in honors club —"

Paul patted his mouth, pretending to yawn.

"And I'm on the soccer team," Holly finished. She'd saved that detail for last in order for it to actually have some impact.

"Wait a second. You play soccer, too?" Paul asked. "Why didn't you say so before?"

"I don't know." Holly shrugged. "You didn't ask? It didn't come up, I guess." *Probably because you were too busy telling me how to fill a squirty ketchup bottle. In detail.*

"Yeah, but you knew *I* played," Paul replied.

"That's because your duffel bag says Southwest Soccer, your T-shirt says Southwest Soccer. . . ." *Plus I'd heard or seen your name before, in the paper.*

Paul laughed. "Pretty boring, huh?" He leaned

against the refrigerator. "So, how come I've never seen you play before?" he asked.

"Maybe because we go to different schools?" Holly said. "I mean, I've never seen you play, either." *Okay, probably I have, since I've been to a lot of Southwest games, and I vaguely recall you being carried around by your teammates, but I'm not going to admit it now,* she thought.

Paul opened a bag of napkins and refilled the metal container on the counter. "Yeah, but I haven't read about you in the paper."

Holly rolled her eyes. "Just because my name wasn't in the paper doesn't mean I'm not on the team."

"No, true." He sprayed the counter and wiped it clean. "Do you start?" he asked.

"Yes, I start." *Is it just me, or was that a really obnoxious question?* "I'm one of the starting fullbacks."

"What? No way." Paul shook his head. "You're too small to be a fullback."

Was he going to argue reality with her now? Like . . . he knew whether she was on the team better than *she* did? "I'm not talking about football. It's soccer," she said.

"I know that. I was just saying that usually, fullbacks are sort of tall."

"Well, I'm tall enough," Holly said.

When he didn't look impressed, she added, "I made varsity when I was a freshman."

"Huh. Funny I've never heard of you," Paul said. "Then again, East's sports record isn't that great, is it?"

"Maybe that's because we spend more time studying," Holly shot back. The rivalry between the two schools usually came down to athletics vs. academics.

"Ooh." Paul pretended to be wounded, holding his stomach as if he'd been punched. "Cruel."

"And maybe the newspaper doesn't cover our school as well as yours," Holly argued. "Or maybe it doesn't cover the girls' teams as much as the boys' teams."

"Okay already!" Paul backed up, holding his hands in mock surrender. "Lighten up."

"You don't have to be the top scorer to contribute to the team, you know." Holly knew she was going overboard, but she couldn't really stop herself.

"Defensive much?" Paul picked up his soda cup and rattled the leftover ice in the bottom of it.

"I'm sure you're great. I mean, if you can defend the goal the way you defend yourself . . . you must have shutouts."

"Shut up." But Holly laughed. "We do. Actually. Not that anyone ever *knows* about them, apparently."

After a lull, more customers came up to order food. They worked side by side for a while without speaking. But all of a sudden, Holly noticed Paul hovering by her elbow, watching her make a club sandwich.

"Not the toast again?" she asked.

"Okay, that's *way* too many pickles. And when you put the toothpick in to hold everything together, you should use the same color for each half."

Holly had stuck a green toothpick in one side and a red in the other. "Why?"

"Then people know that's their sandwich," Paul said, as if it were perfectly obvious.

"What are they going to do, leave it for an hour and then come back?" She looked him in the eye as she stabbed two more toothpicks into each half: one green, one blue, one pink, and one yellow. "Darcy!" she called out, and a girl came up to pick up her sandwich.

"Cute! Look at all those!" she said. "Thanks!"

Holly turned to Paul with a smile. "I think it worked out okay."

"That's not the way we do it," Paul said.

"Maybe not, but that's the way *I* do it." Holly heard herself and had to laugh. She couldn't believe she was having an argument about toothpicks.

"Fine. Whatever," Paul said. "But you know, while we're talking about stuff, we actually cut the lemons like this." He picked up the knife on the cutting board and made a slice going the opposite direction.

Holly couldn't see what the difference was. "Okay, but does it matter that much? It's still a slice of lemon."

"Yes, but this one's easier to squeeze."

"Yes, but this one exposes more lemon to the tea."

He let out an exasperated sigh, sounding disgusted with her. "Okay, whatever, do it your way."

Does he really care that much about a lemon? Then again . . . do I?

"How did you get this job, anyway? Have you ever done this before?" Paul asked.

"How did you get so rude, anyway?" Holly muttered under her breath.

"What?"

"Sure, I've done this before. I cook at home all the time."

"By cook . . . you mean, like, nuke?"

"No. Actually, we have a big family, and we cook a lot," Holly said. "And no offense, but the menu here is not exactly challenging. Grilled cheese? Burgers? A salad that is basically lettuce with one tomato slice?"

"Well, like, what are some of the things you make?"

"I don't know. Pasta, chicken. I bake cakes from scratch." He didn't look impressed. "What are you, the Naked Chef all of a sudden or something?"

"Who?" Paul asked.

Holly shook her head. "Never mind. How did *you* get the job here?"

"My aunt owns a restaurant," he said proudly.

"So why don't you work there?"

"Because this is more fun. Or it's supposed to be." Paul gave her a stone cold look. "Because you can hang out with your friends and use the club and pool and all. Although right now that stuff is not seeming all that important."

"Likewise," Holly said. "In fact, working at a hot dog cart in the middle of the mall sounds better."

"They don't have hot dog carts at the mall."

"Fine. Whatever."

A couple of customers approached the window. Holly turned to Paul. "Go ahead, since you know what you're doing and I don't."

"No, you go ahead. You need the practice," Paul said.

"No, you," Holly insisted. *Great. We used to fight over what orders to take — now we're fighting over not taking them!*

"Isn't it time for your break, anyway?" Paul asked.

"I think it's past time!" Holly tossed her apron on the counter and stormed out.

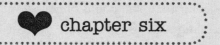

chapter six

Holly marched through the club and headed right to the tennis office. She peeked inside, but it was vacant. She looked out at the courts. She had to talk to Ainslee. When she told Ainslee what a jerk Paul was being, Ainslee would find something funny in the situation, and then she could laugh about it. Laughing at Paul was what she needed to do.

Naturally, when she walked out onto the tennis courts, Ainslee wasn't there, but Ross was — all by himself. *Does he have any students? Besides me, that is?* Holly wondered.

The other courts were filled with players in matches, but Ross was just practicing his serve. He bounced the ball exactly the same way, exactly three times, before tossing it into the air for his serve.

Ross let out a scream as he hit the ball, and Holly just stood there, openmouthed, watching the serve whiz across the net and the ball bounce against the fence faster than she could blink. She couldn't imagine being able to return one of his serves.

"Nice!" She clapped as she walked a little bit closer, intending to ask where Ainslee was.

"Holly! Hey, how's it going?" Ross replied.

"Fine. You know, Ainslee does that, too," she told him.

"Does what?" Ross asked.

"Yells when she hits a good shot. Plus the ball bouncing thing," Holly said.

"The what?" Ross looked confused.

"How you bounce the ball three times before every serve," Holly explained.

"I do? No, I don't," Ross said.

"Okay . . ." Holly said slowly.

"But Ainslee does? Yeah, I guess she does," Ross said. "Cool. Hey, you want to just hit for a while?"

"Sure, okay," Holly said. "I don't have much time, though."

"Then just grab a racket from that bin over there," Ross told her. "I'm sure you can find one with your grip size."

Holly sorted through until she found a racquet she liked. "Actually, I was looking for Ainslee," she said as she came onto the court, racket in hand.

"I figured. She ditched early. Her mom called and she had to go all of a sudden —"

"Was it an emergency?" Holly asked. "Why didn't she come and tell me?"

"It wasn't an emergency. She just had to leave, and she didn't have any lessons, so I said okay." Ross shrugged. "Anyway, now that you're here, let's play."

Holly was curious about what had made Ainslee leave, but she figured it was probably one of her mom's whims. She hit the ball back and forth with Ross for about ten minutes. She wasn't sure why, but he kept praising her. Maybe because she was wailing on the ball because she was still so annoyed with Paul.

"Nice forehand! Wow. Nice shot!" Ross said. "Whoa. Look out. Nice. You dusted the corner lines. Holly, you've gotten a lot better already. So, what do you think — do you want to work on your serve, work up to playing some matches?"

Was he drinking too many Red Bulls or

spending too much time in the sun or something? "No. See, Ross, I'm not that good, so I doubt I'll be playing any matches —"

"You could," Ross interrupted. "And I bet you could make the school team, if you wanted. It's all a matter of perception. Attitude." He tapped his head, looking very serious for a second. Of course, that was hard to do because he was actually tapping his headband, which was kind of funny.

"No, Ainslee and I have been friends for years, and I know how much she practices," Holly said.

"Ainslee is a great player. That's true. How did she get so good, do you think?" Ross asked.

"It's just a guess, but, um, lessons?" Holly suggested.

"No, lessons can only do so much. If you've ever seen her zone in on her approach shot . . ." He shook his head. "*Man.* And I'd kill for her overhead lob."

Lob. That's a good thing, right? Before Ross could toss out any more tennis talk — or impossible shots — Holly thought she should probably get back to work. "Yeah. Right. Well, I should go — I'm only on a fifteen-minute break."

"Okay, thanks for playing," Ross said, as if this

were a game show and he was the host. "See you at your next lesson!" he called after Holly.

When did I go from having lessons with Ainslee to lessons with Ross on a permanent basis? Holly wondered as she jogged back to the café.

"How was tennis?" Paul asked when she walked into the kitchen.

Holly quickly washed her hands at the sink. "How did you know I was playing tennis?"

"Well, I figured you and Ainslee —"

"Actually, I was playing with Ross, not Ainslee. Ever seen him play? He's incredibly good. His serve must be about a hundred miles an hour."

Paul didn't look impressed. "You have green fuzz on your pocket."

Holly lifted the tennis ball fuzz off her shorts and studied it. "Thanks. I need that, actually."

"I can*not* believe my mom made me leave work early to help her go over fabric swatches for a new couch." Ainslee and Holly stood outside the Dairy Creme, waiting in line at their favorite ice-cream place in town at about nine o'clock.

Fortunately the Dairy Creme was close enough to Ainslee's house that they could walk to it and didn't have to ask for a ride. Set just outside the college campus, it was a cool place to hang out both during the school year and the summer.

"So what did you pick?" Holly asked.

"Nothing!" Ainslee threw up her hands. "After all that, now she's not sure she wants a new couch. She says the old one's fine. Which it might possibly have been, if Mr. Whiskers hadn't clawed it to death."

Ainslee and Holly both studied the list of flavors and options for a minute.

"What are you getting?" Ainslee asked. "I think I'm going for the banana fudge swirl. In a shake."

"Speaking of guys," Holly began.

"Were we?"

"Sure. Mr. Whiskers is a guy. Sort of."

"He *was*, anyway," Ainslee said with a laugh. "Okay . . ."

"I was wondering. Do you and Ross get along?" Holly asked. "I mean, how do you like working with him?"

"What do you mean, *with* him? I don't see him much at all."

"You don't?" Holly found that hard to believe. "Don't you share that little office?"

"Yeah, but we're hardly ever in it. We're both

pretty busy. We run into each other sometimes, in passing, but that's almost it."

"Oh. Well, I went over to look for you this afternoon. Ross and I started hitting the ball, and he was trying to tell me that I could be good," Holly said. "He's kind of weird."

Ainslee's brow creased as she looked at Holly. "Why is that weird? You're good at other sports, so you could be."

"I don't know. He sort of acts like he wants to be friends or something," Holly said.

"Okay. So?"

"So, I don't know. Why does he want to be friends with me?" asked Holly.

"I think *you're* the one that's weird. Isn't the whole purpose of working at the club to meet new people and kind of expand our little circle?" Ainslee asked.

"Circle of two? Ains, how can two make a circle?" Holly said.

"Shut up, you know what I mean."

"Then why don't *you* work on being friends with Ross? That makes more sense, because you guys actually have stuff in common. Like talent," Holly said. "Plus he always asks about you and talks about how great a player you are."

"He does? Huh. He hardly ever talks to me at all," Ainslee said.

"Maybe he's shy," Holly suggested, though that didn't seem true. She stepped up to the window to order. It was odd to be on the other side of a takeout window. For a second she wondered what it was like to work at the Dairy Creme — were obnoxious guys working in their kitchen, too? Probably.

"Hot fudge sundae waffle cone, please," Holly said politely. She stepped to the side and waited for her order. When she got her cone and turned around, she saw Paul and a group of guys wearing Southwest Soccer gear standing about ten places back in line.

"What are you doing here?" Holly asked, stopping briefly as she walked past him.

Paul looked at her as if she were crazy. "I always come here."

"No, I always do," Holly insisted.

"Then how come I've never seen you here before?" Paul asked.

Ainslee stepped up behind Holly. "Maybe because you didn't know us? Your loss."

"Whatever." Paul pointed to the giant waffle

cone in Holly's hands. "Do you think that's big enough?"

"Are you just jealous because you're still in line?" Holly asked him. She stuck a spoon into the cone and took a bite. "Anyway, I'm hungry."

"I hope so," Paul said.

"I went running, okay? Not that you need to know, but we ran six miles after work," Holly said. Maybe that would impress him, since nothing else she did really seemed to.

"Really? And how long did it take you?" Paul said. "Because I did a 10K recently in, like, thirty-eight minutes."

"Oh, yeah? Well, we were already done, *showered*, and standing here in line by thirty-eight minutes." Ainslee smiled at Paul, then took a sip of her milk shake. "But, you know. That's just us. Your results may vary."

"I'm sure," Paul muttered, as his friends laughed — mostly at him, it seemed. "You guys are not that fast."

"You want to race sometime and find out?" Ainslee offered. "It's okay. You can get back to us." She nudged Holly's shoulder, encouraging her to move on.

Holly followed Ainslee to a table by the edge of the outdoor seating. "Ains, maybe *you* should work with him, you can keep up better."

"Why does he want to one-up us?" Ainslee asked as she sat down. "I mean, we're . . . not even in competition with him. How does he have any friends? He must constantly be telling them how great he is."

"No doubt," Holly agreed. She snuck a glance over at Paul. "Do you know how hard it is to stand beside someone so good-looking and so rude for eight hours a day?" she asked in a soft voice.

"Well. Not really. I mean, Ross is good-looking," Ainslee mused. "If you could think of him wearing something besides his goofy tennis clothes. He has this hideous white vest that he wears in the morning when we play warm-up. Remember *The Great Gatsby*? Like, he thinks we're in it. And it's a hundred years ago."

"Maybe he's just trying to blend in with the club's décor. Not that there were headbands a hundred years ago. Were there?" Holly asked, and they both giggled. "Anyway, so Ross has weird taste in clothes, but you don't want to *kill* him."

Ainslee laughed. "No. Not yet, anyway."

Holly kept an eye on Paul, who was moving up

in line, getting close to ordering. He'd probably tell the people at Dairy Creme how to fill an ice-cream cone.

"Maybe we're just jealous of Ross because we don't have a signature piece," Holly said. "You know how people are known for things. What are *we* going to be known for?"

"You're way too philosophical for the Dairy Creme. But if you want, you can be known for that," Ainslee offered.

Holly laughed, then watched as Paul and his friends grabbed a table on the other side of the patio. They'd only been sitting there a minute when a blond girl with long, tanned legs walked up to their picnic table. She slid onto the bench, right next to Paul. He was in the middle of saying something, and everyone at the table cracked up laughing. Holly watched as the girl leaned against Paul.

"Well, so much for sixteen being lucky," she mumbled.

"What do you mean?" asked Ainslee.

"Look." Holly gestured with her chin. "It's that girl who works in the spa —"

"Who?" Ainslee stared across the patio. "Oh, yeah. Teri."

"Anyway, she's beautiful. And look at how close she's sitting to Paul."

"*Anyway*, you're not sixteen yet," Ainslee said. "And *anyway*, you just said you couldn't stand Paul, so why do you care?"

It was true, Holly thought. She couldn't stand Paul. At least, not most of the time.

The other part of the time . . . she couldn't stand standing next to him, because it made her nervous.

Fine. So he was taken. Fine. She'd get over it.

In fact, she already was over it.

Maybe the lucky part about being sixteen was not making mistakes by hooking up with the wrong person. If she was looking for a fling that summer, she'd just have to start looking somewhere else. Outside the kitchen. Which would make work so much easier, really.

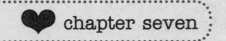

chapter seven

"So, you want to take a break?" Paul asked the next day at work, at about eleven-twenty.

Holly shook her head as she refilled the napkin dispenser. "No."

"You sure?"

"Yes. We just got here," Holly said.

"Yeah, I know, I just thought maybe you want to check in with Ainslee or something. Go for a quick marathon run."

"Ha-ha," Holly said. "Funny."

"Thanks. You guys are really into running, huh?"

"Some . . . times," Holly said slowly. What was he doing, trying to make polite conversation? That wasn't like him. *He's probably being nice and offering me a break because he wants to ask for some extra time off later. So he can go see Teri and have a spa back rub. Ew.*

"Anyway, how could you even suggest I leave

now? It's your famous lunch rush. Unless . . . *you* wanted to take a break?" she asked.

"No, I'm cool," Paul said.

In your own mind, anyway, Holly thought as she watched him create a sandwich out of a burger, some turkey, and about four slices of cheese.

He looked up and caught Holly watching him. "Hungry? Since it's dead right now, you should eat, too," he suggested.

She hated to agree with him, but he had a point. If she didn't eat now she'd end up having to wait until two or later.

She quickly made a club sandwich, putting a layer of sliced dill pickles on the top and the bottom. As she sliced it in half, she noticed Paul had stopped eating and was just watching her. "What are you looking at?"

"How many pickles actually *fit* on a sandwich?" Paul asked.

"I like pickles. Sue me." Holly filled a cup with root beer and leaned against the counter to eat her sandwich.

"You have weird taste," Paul commented.

No doubt, Holly thought. *That's obviously why I*

kind of still find you attractive, even though you can be such an obnoxious jerk.

Paul walked closer to her. "What did you just say?"

Oh, no, did I say any part of that aloud? Kill me. Now. Before I die of embarrassment. "Nothing!" Holly insisted. "I was just mumbling."

"Knock knock." Russell stood in the doorway. "What are you, having lunch together?"

Holly and Paul looked at each other. "No," Holly said.

"We just happened to, uh, see a slow moment," Paul explained, "and so we thought we'd grab a bite —"

"It's dead, isn't it? We should be busier. I know. Our lunch sales are down this year," Russell said, sounding a little dejected.

"Really." Paul looked at Holly with raised eyebrows.

"What? It's not *me*," she whispered fiercely.

"Slightly down. One-half percent so far," Russell continued. "Still, it concerns me, so I came by to see how things are going. You two doing all right? You two having any problems?"

You mean, like the fact that I want to kill him

half of the time, and kiss him the other half of the time? Russell was way too old to understand what that was like — even if she told him, which she wouldn't, especially not with Paul standing right beside her.

"Nope. No problems," Holly said cheerfully to her boss.

"Paul?" Russell prompted. "How about you?"

Please don't tell him that I use too much ketchup and too many pickles, Holly thought. *Or whatever else you think of me.*

"Not really," Paul agreed.

"Oh, good," Russell sighed. "I hate it when there are problems. I can't handle problems."

In Holly's humble opinion, Russell didn't sound like the perfect person to be a kitchen manager. Weren't managers supposed to know how to handle stressful situations?

"Not like last year, right?" Paul asked.

Russell shook his head. "That was a nightmare. I thought we'd never get through in one piece."

"What happened?" Holly asked.

"Paul was the only reliable employee. By a country mile. First we had three people working here. Then one of them just stopped showing up one day. Then she came back. Then she'd be here one day and not the next. So we fired her," Russell explained. "In the meantime, the other girl kept trying to change her hours, because she got another job."

Holly glanced sideways at Paul. Had he driven both of them away? Was Russell even considering the fact that his biggest problem might be standing right here?

"So she eventually left, then we got a replacement — a guy. Well." Russell shook his head. "*He* couldn't even make a peanut-butter-and-jelly sandwich."

"He couldn't even fill a glass of water without asking how!" Paul added.

"Clueless. Exactly." Russell grabbed a sponge and scrubbed at a burn spot on the stove. "We're counting on you, Holly. You have no idea how much."

Nothing like being asked to make up for other people's mistakes, Holly thought. No wonder Paul was so critical — and so used to being right all the time. He'd had to shoulder a lot the previous summer. Then again, it wasn't rocket science, the way he acted sometimes. And maybe his attitude was so irritating that people just pretended not to be able to make PB&J sandwiches.

"Anyhoo." Russell pointed outside, where a crowd of about twenty small children was filing straight from the pool toward their window, towels around their shoulders, trailing water on the patio. "Here they come. Here come our little eaters. Paul, get the dogs grilling!"

Holly tossed what was left of her sandwich and washed her hands as a line formed at the window. So this was the famous lunch rush.

"Well. That'll help the bottom line," Russell said a couple of hours later, when business finally slowed down. "Isn't it time for your tennis lesson?" he asked Holly. "Shoo, shoo."

"Right. Tennis." Just the thought of playing made Holly want to lie down and fall asleep. Maybe she shouldn't have run so far the night before. "But, ah, maybe you need me to stay here."

"Don't think so. But thanks!" Paul said with a smile. "See ya!"

She faked a smile and waved good-bye. "Buh-bye!"

He couldn't wait to get rid of her. And she couldn't wait to have a break from him and his . . . happiness. He'd been so bubbly all day, and she was sure it all had to do with his date the night before.

Happiness was so disgusting in other people.

Holly took the long way to the tennis courts, passing by the club's spa on her way. She peered in the window on the top half of the door. Teri was sitting at the front desk, painting her fingernails.

Tough job, thought Holly, *but somebody's got to do it*.

"Ross? Not to make a big deal out of this?" she said when she found him at the courts. He was lying on the bench, his face to the sky, sunning himself. "But I could hardly move when I got up this morning. So maybe we could take it easy today?"

"No problem. I'm really beat today, anyway. I went to a concert last night in Columbus." Ross yawned and stretched his arms over his head, nearly falling off the bench. "I was up until two."

"Who did you see?"

"Foo Fighters."

"You're kidding. You should have told Ainslee. That's one of her favorite bands, too."

"Are you serious?" Ross rubbed his eyes underneath his sunglasses.

Holly nodded. Of course, Ainslee's mom probably wouldn't have let her go, but Ross didn't need to know that. "She has all their songs on her MP3."

"Huh. Maybe I should have asked her to go," Ross said. "You think she would have come?"

"Maybe. Anyway, speaking of. Where is she now?" asked Holly.

Ross sat up and slowly got to his feet. "She said something about a training session in the gym. You know what? Let's work on your serve today," he said as he grabbed his racket.

Holly stared at him. "But Ross, I don't *have* a serve."

He smiled. "Exactly. Come on. Wow. Ainslee and the Foo Fighters, huh."

When Holly got back to the café after a quick shower and clothes change, Ainslee was leaning against the counter, eating a frozen fruit bar and talking to Paul. They were laughing.

Strange. The only time she'd ever seen Paul laughing, it was at *her*.

"Yeah, but have you noticed the weight room?"

Paul was saying. "The machines are, like, thirty years old. Nobody even knows how to use them."

"That's nothing — have you seen that giant cobweb right over the stationary bike?" Ainslee laughed. "The one with the pedals that go around and around like a ghost is pushing them?"

"Oh, so now the weight room is haunted?" Paul scoffed.

"Yes, by the sweat of . . . well, ick, who knows," Ainslee said, and they laughed again.

Holly stepped up to the counter and leaned against Ainslee. "So now there are ghost stories about this place?"

"Hey! I came by to visit," Ainslee said. "Where have you been?"

"I had my tennis lesson." Holly looked at Paul. "Didn't you tell her? You know, the one they said I couldn't schedule with you because you were too busy?" Holly said.

"Oh. Well, I just got here, actually," Ainslee said. "I wasted my break looking for *you*."

"Wasted? Thanks," Paul muttered.

"Oh, come on!" Ainslee laughed. "Don't take it personally."

"You *wish* you had something better to do with your break," Paul said.

"Oh, yeah, that's it, exactly." Ainslee tossed her Popsicle stick at him. "Quelle big head we have."

"What?"

"Never mind, it's French. You wouldn't understand," Ainslee said.

"I wouldn't," Paul said. "But funny, it didn't sound French."

"It's her accent," Holly said.

"Better work on it, then," Paul said.

"So, have you been here long?" Holly asked once Paul had disappeared into the back of the kitchen, out of sight.

"Long enough," Ainslee said. "I totally have the scoop. Come on."

"But I'm kind of late —"

"Give me three minutes," Ainslee urged. "Come over here — we need a little more privacy."

Holly followed her to the edge of the patio. "So what did you find out?"

"Check it out. Remember how we thought Paul might be dating that girl we saw at the Dairy Creme last night —"

"Teri."

"Teri. Exactly," Ainslee said. "Well, while I was standing there waiting for my Popsicle, because I

90

had to order something or I'd look really pathetic, Teri came by — with Toby. She's dating Toby, not Paul. Isn't that great?"

Holly wasn't sure why that made Ainslee so happy. Was she supposed to be happy about it, too? "I don't care that Teri's not his girlfriend," she said.

"Don't you?" Ainslee asked. "I thought you liked him."

"Liked," Holly said. "Past tense. Before I met him."

"Anyway, I didn't want to find out just for you. I wanted to know for my sake," Ainslee said. "Since you're not that into him. Right?"

Holly shrugged. "Right."

Ainslee peeked over her shoulder at Paul waiting on a customer. "Who knows? He might even be the perfect summer fling for me."

Holly couldn't quite believe what she was hearing. "Ains. Are you serious? Have you spent any time with him?"

"I just have to find out a little more about him. Like, just because he's not seeing Teri, that doesn't mean he doesn't have a girlfriend, I guess," Ainslee mused. "Wait. I know! Has he been on his cell phone constantly?"

Holly thought about it for a minute. "No. He's had a few calls, maybe."

"Well, there you go," Ainslee declared. "Guys with girlfriends are on the phone all the time. And vice versa."

"Even at work? Is that why I have leftover minutes?" Holly quipped.

"Think about your sisters! Didn't your parents go nuts because Arianna's cell phone bill was so high —"

"Three hundred dollars," Holly said.

"Right. Because she was talking to what's-his-name constantly."

"She got grounded for two weeks, then my parents got that 'everything included all the time' calling plan because the whole time she was grounded, she was still calling Brad. Or was it Blaine? Anyway."

"When I date someone? I for sure won't be like that," Ainslee said.

Holly laughed. "You won't?"

"Nope. All desperate and inseparable? No way."

"I don't know, I think it looks sort of fun," Holly mused. "Isn't that what being in love is supposed to feel like? Like you can't live without the other person?"

"Only if you're Juliet and he's Romeo. And then it's true, no, you can't live without him, because you're both dead."

"You're such a romantic."

Ainslee glanced at her watch. "Oh, shoot. It's time to teach my six-year-olds. Okay, so — find out what you can while you're working, okay? About Paul?"

"Sure, but I already know everything I need to," Holly said. "He's a conceited know-it-all —"

"Oh, come on, lighten up. He's not that bad. And have you looked at the guy's eyes? Gorgeous. See you later!" Ainslee called over her shoulder as she jogged off toward the tennis court.

Holly went back into the kitchen. *Look at his eyes*, she told herself. *Do it for Ainslee's sake.*

Yes, they were still very nice.

"So exactly how long did you plan on working today?" Paul asked. "Two hours, or three?"

And yes, he was still rude.

"Don't worry — I'll make up for the extra break time. I'll do all the dishes," Holly volunteered.

"So? You were going to do them all, anyway," Paul said.

"I was?" Holly asked.

"Sure. Seniority."

Holly gave him a skeptical look. "Russell didn't mention anything about seniority."

Paul put away a set of stacked mixing bowls. "That's because it's assumed. And he was too busy freaking out about nothing. He has a habit of doing that."

Holly filled up the sink with hot water and dish soap. If what Ainslee said was true, and he wasn't seeing Teri, then was he really free to date? But why did she care? Why would she want to go out with him, when he was so obnoxious all the time?

But he wasn't obnoxious all *the time*, Holly thought. That was the thing. Sometimes he was kind of nice and semisweet and slightly funny.

Paul came over to stand beside her at the sink. He dropped a few forks and spoons into the soapy water. "So, what are you doing this weekend?" he asked.

"Besides working here?" Holly replied.

"Well, yeah."

"I'm not sure," Holly said. *Try to think of*

something mysterious and important-sounding. "I actually have a couple of options. Why?"

"There's this party Saturday night," Paul said.

Oh my God, is he about to ask me out? To a party with him? "Really? What party?"

"Russell was talking about it. Eight o'clock, at Mrs. Whittingham's," Paul said.

"Oh," Holly sighed.

"You were hoping for something cooler?" he asked.

"Kind of," Holly admitted. "What's the party for?"

"All the employees. In appreciation for the first couple weeks of work," Paul said.

"She sure has a lot of parties," Holly commented.

"Yeah," Paul agreed. "She does."

Holly rinsed a couple of dishes and set them in the drying rack. "So. You think you'll go?" she asked, trying to make it sound like she didn't care.

"I don't know. Probably," Paul said. "Depends on what else is going on. How about you?"

Holly shrugged. "Maybe. See what else comes up." Not that anything better *would*, but she wasn't about to admit that to him.

"So maybe I'll see you there," Paul said.

"Sure. Maybe you will." Holly looked over at him as he cleaned the refrigerator shelves. She'd have to tell Ainslee that he was an obsessive neat freak.

With nice eyes.

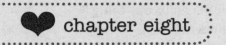

chapter eight

"Come on. Play badminton with me."

Holly looked at Ross, who was standing in front of her holding out a racket. She was sitting on the steps leading from Mrs. Whittingham's large porch on Saturday night.

"Badminton. You're not serious," she said.

"Sure I am. It's fun," Ross said. "Plus, it's good practice for your hand-eye coordination, which will help with your tennis."

Didn't he understand that she really didn't want to get any better at tennis? Should she just come out and tell him that the only reason she signed up for lessons was to hang out with Ainslee? But that sounded stupid.

"Ross, I have a question. Why are you trying to turn me into racquet sports girl this summer?" Holly asked.

"Simple. You can be my protégé," Ross said.

"No, I can't," Holly argued. "Protégés have to be younger than fifteen, for one thing."

"You're only fifteen?"

"I'll be sixteen in a week, but yeah. Why, do I look older?" She kind of hoped he would say, *Yes. You seem at least twenty.*

He shrugged. "I don't know. I guess I thought since you're going to be a junior, you were older."

"Why? How old are you?"

"Seventeen," he said.

"And how long have *you* been playing tennis?" Holly asked.

"Since I was eight," Ross replied.

"There you go. I rest my case."

Ross sat down beside her. "I was sort of joking about the protégé thing, okay? But just because you're sort of still new to tennis, that doesn't mean you can't get good. You've come a long way just in the past couple of weeks."

Holly narrowed her eyes as she looked at him. "You have some ulterior motive. Do you get a bonus if I get voted most improved or something?"

"No, I don't," Ross said. "Well, maybe I could, but I just hate to see wasted potential —"

"Ross. Come on," Holly said. "Tell the truth."

Ross sighed. "All right, fine. There's this mixed doubles competition at the end of the season. And it's kind of a big deal. The club players take on, like, everyone who signs up. And it's expected that they do really well," he explained.

"So, ask Ainslee to be your partner. You guys are the club players. Obviously." In fact, Holly wasn't sure why Ainslee hadn't mentioned it to her yet. She loved competitions like that — any excuse to compete would do, when it came to tennis.

"I know, but the thing is that Ainslee, uh, well, she doesn't seem to like me. All that much. So I thought maybe you could talk to her for me, you know, tell her how I've been helping you, and —"

"What? She does too like you," Holly said, although she wasn't sure Ainslee had ever really moved beyond thinking Ross was a bit strange and a bit headband-obsessed. "And she likes winning, so why wouldn't she team up with you?"

"For spite?" Ross suggested. "She's mad at me because I tried to help her with her volleys. All I said was that she needed to step into the shot more, you know? And go for the angles. If you're at the net, you need to put it away."

"Oh, yeah. That's what *I* always try to do," Holly joked. Out of the corner of her eye, Holly noticed some heat lightning flashing in the sky. "Do you think it'll storm tonight?" she asked Ross.

"Probably. Anyway, do you think Ainslee will forgive me?" Ross asked.

"Oh, yeah. I'm sure Ainslee will get over it." Holly smiled politely, thinking, *Probably not all that soon, actually.* Ainslee could hold a grudge, and she hated being criticized — even if the criticism was well meant.

"Could you maybe talk to her for me? Or something?" Ross asked. "Put in a good word?"

Holly was starting to wonder if this was about more than the upcoming tournament. "Sure. Of course." Holly decided she'd better go find out from Ainslee what was going on. "In fact, I'll start just as soon as I get something to drink," she told Ross as she stood up, stretching her arms above her head.

"Okay, see you around," he said, as he turned in the direction of his friends.

Holly walked over to the large punch bowl. Paul jogged over with his friends just as she had finished filling her cup with lemonade, except in a clear cup it looked slightly green.

"What's that?" Toby asked, pointing at the bowl.

"Retro-ade," Paul said.

"Retro-ade?" Holly asked.

"This stuff is left over from five years ago and they're still using it up. They've been serving it at all the parties," Paul said.

"Come on, dude," said Toby. "You're making that up."

"Let me ask you. Did you guys drink lemonade at the welcome party a couple of weeks ago?" Paul looked at Toby and Holly.

Holly remembered the bitter taste the lemonade had left in her mouth. "Well . . . yes?"

"And did you notice that it tasted kind of strange?"

Toby nodded.

"That was the taste of Retro-ade."

"Or do you mean radioactive-ade?" Holly set down her half-full cup. "What's it really called?"

"ILSR. Intense Lemon Sport Refreshment."

"Hmm. Catchy name," Holly commented. "I wonder why it didn't take off. Well, besides the semiputrid taste."

Toby laughed. "No doubt that was a problem."

"Haven't you ever noticed the giant cans of mix in the pantry?" Paul asked her.

"I tend not to linger in the pantry. I'm too busy running to get stuff," Holly said.

"Oh, yeah, right," Paul scoffed. "Because you're working so hard all the time."

Holly laughed. "I am!"

"Then how come I caught you staring out at the pool twice yesterday?" Paul asked.

"Am I not allowed to take a break now and then?" Holly said. "I was wondering if we could start offering poolside service, like at the fancier clubs. In the movies."

Paul just kept looking at her, as if he wanted to say something else.

"What?" Holly said.

"If we did, do you really think you'd be the first choice for the job? I mean, we've *seen* your poolside work," he teased. "Shrimp puff?"

He and Toby headed back over to the shuffleboard court, laughing and carrying extra cups of lemonade for their buddies.

Holly wondered whether Mrs. Whittingham had a game of darts handy. The kind with sharp metal tips. She had a target in mind.

She stared into her cup of ILSR and then tossed it into the trash can.

She walked past the badminton net, where Ainslee and Ross were competing against two girls. Ainslee kept swinging her badminton racquet like a tennis racquet. "Got it!" she cried, nearly knocking Ross in the face.

Ross was looking at her as if he didn't care whether she smashed him or not.

Poor Ross, Holly thought. He was interested in Ainslee, and all she was interested in was winning.

"I think Mrs. Whittingham is lonely," Ainslee mused as they sat down to eat. There were two long folding tables set up under a white tent on her lawn. Holly still couldn't get over how well Mrs. Whittingham treated all of them.

"What makes you say that?" she asked.

"Well, this is the second time she's had us all over to her house," Ainslee said. "I was talking to her earlier and she said something about how much she misses her grandkids."

"Where are they?" Holly took a bite of barbecued chicken.

"Grown up. They're, like, thirty now, or something. She's a great-grandmother now."

"She looks pretty good, considering her age. She plays great badminton, anyway."

"No kidding. Better than Paul," Ainslee commented. "You totally had his back when you were on the same side. You know what?" Ainslee leaned across the table and whispered, "I'm kind of jealous. You guys really have chemistry."

"Us? Chemistry?" *If that meant things were about to explode, then yes. But not in a good way.* "No," Holly laughed. "It's like he can't resist getting digs in at me. No matter where we are or what we're doing, he'll find a way. Do you know what he said when we were playing over there? He said, 'You put the *bad* in *badminton.*'"

Ainslee chewed on a plastic fork. "Still. My mom says chemistry is the most important thing in a relationship. Without it, you're sunk."

"Chemistry's important, I guess," Holly agreed. "But it's not the only thing. Like, the person also has to not be a jerk. I'm actually thinking of asking Russell if he can find someone else to work in the kitchen. I think I need a different job."

"Seriously?" asked Ainslee.

"Well, not that seriously. But I do want to talk to him about stuff," Holly said.

"Okay, while you're doing that, I'm going to ask Paul if he's free," Ainslee said.

"Free?"

"Like, available. To date," Ainslee explained.

"What? No, you're not," Holly replied.

Ainslee nodded. "I am."

"Are not."

"Why?"

"Because! It'll seem like you're asking for me!" Holly whispered.

"Are you joking? You guys can't stand each other. Everyone can see that. You haven't gotten along since day one, when he almost poked out your eye and you —"

"Fell into the pool. I know. He was just reminding me," Holly said.

"So, as you can see, it'll be obvious I'm asking for *me*," Ainslee argued. "Which I am."

"You are?" Holly asked, surprised.

"Well, yeah. He's still Extremely Cute Guy, and we're only talking about a fling, remember? Someone to have fun with over the summer?"

"Okay, but if you're looking for someone to

have fun with . . . do you really think Paul fits that description? What about, uh, Ross?"

"Ross?" Ainslee wrinkled her nose, as if Holly had just suggested something bizarre.

"Any chemistry there?" asked Holly.

Ainslee seemed to be thinking it over for a minute. "He's not horrible. I guess. Why, are you thinking about asking him out? Ooh, look, there's Paul — got to go."

Holly couldn't help thinking that things were getting sort of weird all of a sudden. She cleaned her hands of barbecue sauce and went over to talk to Russell, who was standing at the edge of the tent.

He was gazing up at the sky. "Doesn't look good, does it?"

"Not really," Holly agreed.

"But I'd say we've got an hour before it gets nasty." Russell dropped his empty plate into the trash can.

"Hey, Russell? I have a couple of things I wanted to ask you about," Holly said. *Like: Could you get rid of that really annoying guy I work with?*

"Are there any problems? Because I can't handle problems," Russell replied.

"Not problems, exactly," Holly said, trying to

think how best to phrase this. "More like . . . suggestions."

"Constructive criticism?" asked Russell.

Holly nodded. "Exactly."

"All right, go ahead. You know what? Let's take a walk — I always enjoy visiting Mrs. Whittingham's gardens when I'm here. But remember, Holly — there are no problems without solutions." That was Russell's mantra. For life.

"Okay," Holly said as they headed down a stone path toward the rose garden. "So I was thinking. Um, sometimes it seems like we could offer just a couple more things to eat at the café. They wouldn't be complicated or take a long time to cook or anything. They'd totally fit into our menu but they'd just make it more . . . diverse. Sort of."

Russell stopped to admire a yellow rosebush. "Such as?"

"A Gardenburger. Or some other veggie burger." Holly carefully touched the soft rose petals. "Because a lot of vegetarians come to the club and want to order food and all they can really choose is grilled cheese. Or chips."

"Or salad," Russell said. "We have a salad."

"Well, that's the other thing. Do you think we could make our salad a little more interesting? We need some other lettuce, maybe some carrots, a couple other veggies. Maybe offer more than one kind of salad dressing," Holly suggested. "Then that would be a better option."

Russell narrowed his eyes. "Are you a vegetarian or something?"

"Nope. I just kind of talk to the customers and see what they want. And there are a few who mentioned this stuff, so I said I'd pass it along to you. So what do you think?" Holly asked. "Could we try changing a few things? Actually, it's more like adding, not changing."

They walked along the far side of the garden, past the topiary hedges. "I think you might have a point," Russell said. "I could think of other things for the grill, too. I've always wanted to have a chicken sandwich."

Holly wasn't sure if he meant ordering one, eating one, or offering one. "You have?" she asked, keeping it vague.

"Seems like another natural change. I just haven't wanted to change the traditions."

Since when is a cheeseburger a tradition? Holly wondered.

As she was telling Russell about a few other suggestions, Paul came jogging up to the two of them.

"Russell," he panted. "Don't let her quit."

"Quit? I wasn't quitting." *And do you really care that much?* Usually he acted like he wanted nothing more than to have the kitchen all to himself again.

"Ainslee said you were going to get reassigned."

"No. I never said that." *I may have said something exactly like it, but I wasn't serious.* What was Ainslee trying to do to her? Call her bluff?

Russell suddenly looked very uncomfortable. He pulled at his necktie. "Did you want to get reassigned, Holly?" he asked.

She shook her head. "Oh, no. Not at all."

"I didn't think so, given what we were just talking about. Ah — that reminds me. I need to call Reinhart Foods. I don't have my cell phone on me. Excuse me." Russell made a beeline for the house.

"So what was he talking about?" Paul asked.

There was a rumble of thunder and a flash of lightning. "We should probably go in," said Holly.

"Yeah, okay," Paul agreed, and they started

walking across the huge lawn. "So, remember that first night here? When you fell into the pool?"

"Dove into the pool," Holly corrected him. It might not be true, but it was the version she'd chosen to go with.

"Shrimp puff?" Paul offered.

"Yeah and you were so nice about it. 'Swim much?' That's what you said."

"I did?"

"Yeah."

"Well, you did look kind of stupid. You have to admit. You were holding up this soggy tray and your hair was all wet and plastered to your face —"

There was another clap of thunder, and this one sounded like it was much closer. Holly thought she felt the ground shake.

"The storm's here — what should we do?" Paul yelled, looking around for a safe hiding place.

Holly looked over at the house. Everyone had gone either inside or under the porch awning for protection. And then suddenly she could hardly see the house. Sheets of rain were moving across the expansive lawn, heading right for them.

"Run!" she shouted as the clouds above them opened and rain poured down.

She and Paul started sprinting for the house. Lightning flashed, and another crack of thunder frightened Holly so much that she lost her footing on the slippery wet grass. Paul grabbed her arm to pull her up, then held her hand as they ran for the house again.

Ross dashed down the porch steps toward them with an umbrella. "Here — don't drown!"

"No, it's — I'm okay," Holly said. She dropped Paul's hand and rushed up the stairs to safety.

Up on the porch, she brushed back her wet hair and looked at Paul. He was completely soaked, too.

Their eyes met, and it was like they'd made this connection they never had before.

Something's happening, Holly thought.

But then she wasn't so sure. She'd never felt like this. *Is something happening?*

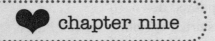

chapter nine

"Can you reach that?" Holly asked.

"What?"

"That saucepan up there." She pointed to the pan hanging on a grid rack over the stove.

"Where?"

"There." She stepped closer to Paul, and felt that sort of weird sparkly feeling she'd had on Saturday night with him. Was it chemistry, or did it mean a thunderstorm was coming?

"Sure." Paul sounded irritated. He was acting as if it were a big imposition, Holly thought. As if being tall was difficult and meant carrying an extra burden through life. Next time, she'd scale the counter and get it herself. She'd probably end up falling, land on top of the grill, and suffer third-degree burns. Not that Paul would care. He'd probably just call out, "Next!"

It was funny. Both of them were acting as if nothing slightly weird and strange had happened three nights ago. But it had. Holly was sure of it. They'd never looked at each other like that before.

And the way things were going? They probably never would again, either.

Holly felt a gentle tap on top of her head.

"Saucepan," he said.

"Thanks." She took the saucepan over to the sink to wash it out, because it looked like it hadn't been used in a while.

Paul followed her. "What do you need it for? What are you making?"

She scrubbed the pan and ran it under hot water. "I'm just heating up some sauerkraut. For the hot dogs." She opened the industrial-size jar.

"Sauerkraut? Do we need that? You're kidding. Think that jar's big enough?" Paul asked.

She shrugged. "I know, but I guess it was the only size they had." Holly emptied about a quarter of the jar into the saucepan with a wooden spoon.

Paul made a face and pinched his nose closed. "It smells horrible," he said in a nasal voice.

"A little strong, maybe, but it'll taste great. If you like sauerkraut," Holly said.

"I don't," said Paul. "Did Russell say you could do that?"

"Of course. He ordered it," Holly said.

"Since when?" asked Paul.

"Since I suggested it on Saturday night."

"Since you what? Wait — you mean, when you were talking to him at the party?"

"Yeah, but I didn't know how much he'd actually go for, so I was kind of surprised —"

"Wait a second. What's that?" Paul asked. He pointed to a black chalkboard that was sitting on the front counter.

"Check out the new menu," Holly said. "The old one, as you know, didn't have enough letters, so I asked him if we could get this and some colored chalk."

Paul turned it to get a better look. "Did you do that?" She nodded. "You have cool handwriting."

"Thanks. Now when we run out of something, we can just cross it off the list, or erase it," Holly pointed out.

Paul looked at her suspiciously. "What are we going to run out of?"

"Who knows. Maybe our new veggie burger?" Holly suggested.

"Wait a second. When did you do all this?" Paul asked. "And you got permission?"

"I talked to Russell. You remember when you

came running out to the gardens and thought I was asking to be transferred?" *And you were sort of panicky about it, acting a little like Russell usually does? And then we got caught in the rain together and you kind of, uh, held my hand?* She could feel her face turning red at the memory. Or else it was that rogue burner.

Paul looked a little bit upset, rather than impressed. "Yeah," he admitted. "But I didn't really think you were leaving."

"Right. Sure," Holly said. "Anyway, that's what we were talking about."

"Why did you do all this?" he asked. "I mean, it's just a stupid grill job."

This from the guy who'd insisted his job was so skilled that she couldn't possibly learn it in a day?

"I don't know. Because I was bored? Because I sit around at night, pathetically without plans, and think about work?" *And usually I think about you first, which is what makes me think about work, but, anyway . . .*

"You do?" Paul asked.

"Well. Sometimes," Holly said. "I was joking about the no-plans thing, though."

"Right."

"Seriously!" she added with a laugh.

"Uh-huh."

"So, come on, try a veggie burger. I'm going to have one." Holly grabbed a couple from the bag in the freezer. She'd never had this brand, and she hoped they were good. She dropped them onto the grill, then got a couple of buns to grill, too. As the burgers cooked, she got out all the condiments.

Paul studied the new menu. "When are you going to tell me how to make all the new stuff?"

"The salad ingredients are right there." She pointed to a cheat sheet she'd made and hung over the prep counter. "Chicken sandwich and veggie burger you just grill, about four minutes a side."

When they were done, Holly took the burgers off the grill. She placed one of them between two halves of a grilled bun on a paper plate, and handed it to Paul. "You're hungry, right? Plus this way you can tell people they're good."

Paul took a bite and chewed it slowly, making a face. "I'm not going to tell anyone that these are good. Yuck. These are disgusting."

"You're not even trying. Put some mustard,

pickles, and banana peppers on top. And some ketchup, too. It's really good that way."

"Hmm." He seemed sort of annoyed, but also interested. "How many pickles? Twenty or thirty?"

"Come on." Holly finished doctoring her veggie burger and took a bite. "Not bad, I'd say."

"Holly! Where were you?"

She looked up and saw Ross standing at the counter. "Um, I'm kind of busy today," she said. "We're rolling out this new menu, so . . ."

"So, nothing." Ross tapped a straw against the counter. "If you don't take the lesson, then I don't get paid."

"Is that really true?" asked Paul.

"No." He shrugged and smiled. "But you should come by and play, anyway."

"Well, we really are kind of busy," Paul said. "I mean, not right now, exactly, but Russell isn't coming in today, so . . ."

"How about tomorrow, Ross?" Holly suggested.

"Okay. Sounds good." He studied the menu for a minute. "Could I just get a Fudgsicle?"

"Sure thing." Holly reached into the freezer and pulled one out. He gave her a dollar, and she handed him the frozen treat.

"So, uh, did you get a chance to talk to Ainslee yet?" Ross asked as he unwrapped it. "About the tournament? And, uh, stuff."

"Well, not exactly, but I will," Holly promised.

"What tournament?" asked Paul.

"I really hope she'll sign up with me. I know we could win," Ross said.

"What tournament? Oh, you mean that mid-summer competition? I'll do it with you," Paul offered.

Ross and Holly started laughing.

Paul glared at them. "What?"

"It's mixed doubles," Ross told him. "Unless you want to wear a skirt?"

Paul glared at him. "Fine."

Holly laughed again. The mental picture of the two guys playing in matching headbands . . . one of them in a skirt . . . was too much.

"Anyway, do you play tennis? A lot? Because we could hit sometime," Ross offered. "Like after work today?"

"I don't have my racket," Paul said. "Anyway, I'm busy."

"Right," Holly said after Ross had left. "You're busy and you don't have your racket."

"What?"

"You're totally afraid of playing him," Holly said. "Which you should be, because he's really good."

"I don't know what you like about that guy," Paul complained. "What do you see in him?"

"I don't see anything," Holly said. What was he getting at — did he think she liked him or something? "He just teaches me tennis. So . . . I see a really good tennis player who might teach me something, which is ironic because I only signed up for lessons so I could hang out with Ainslee."

"Ironic. Whatever," Paul said. "How come you were talking to him so much at the party?"

Holly stared at him. "Jealous much?"

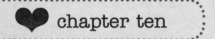

chapter ten

"Why did we ride our bikes today, of all days?"

"Because we were sick of getting rides from our parents," Holly said. "Because we wanted our independence."

"Yeah, well. Independence is totally overrated," Ainslee said as she locked her bike to the rack outside the club. "Quelle mistake. I'm drenched with sweat. Disgusting. I'll have to take a shower before I go play, instead of after."

When Holly and Ainslee walked into the club, instead of the blast of cold air that usually greeted them, the air just felt sort of stuffy and old. There was a sign on the door:

YES. WE KNOW THE A/C IS BROKEN. WE'RE WORKING ON IT. SORRY!

"Recycled air sucks," Ainslee commented. "Literally. Right? It sucks the old air from the vents and sends it around again."

"Like airplane air."

"Très disgusting," Ainslee said.

Holly sighed as she imagined what the next eight hours would be like. Sticky, at best. "Lucky me gets to be in this all day, in a hot kitchen."

"Hey, I have to be outside," Ainslee reminded her. "Where it's ninety-five, which means it's one-oh-five on the court. At least. Probably one-fifteen."

"Right. Sorry."

"We'll probably both lose five pounds in sweat. Do we need to? No."

"Maybe no one will show up to play tennis?" Holly said.

Ainslee raised an eyebrow. "I have the ladies club competition today. I have lessons for six-year-olds. And supposedly someone's coming from some tennis association to check our credentials or credits or something."

"Oh. Well, maybe none of those people will want to eat. They'll be too hot."

"Right. And I'm sure you won't need ice or soda or ice cream, either, because probably no one will be thirsty —"

"All right already!" Holly cried. "I'm going."

She was halfway down the hall when Paul jogged up beside her. "I'm not late," he said.

"No one said you were."

That was just like him, to be competitive about who clocked in first. Not that there was an official clock, because it had broken several years ago.

He unlocked the door. "I'll do inventory and get stuff ready," he said.

"I'll clean up," Holly offered.

They both cleaned the kitchen and ran the dishwasher when they left each shift, but there were always leftover tasks from the day before.

She gave him a sideways glance as she started washing a few dishes that had been left in the sink. "So, did you see the sign about the A/C?" she asked.

"You can tell it's on the fritz because it's already too warm in here."

"The fritz?" Holly laughed. "What's a fritz?"

"It's something my grandparents always say. We make fun of them."

"How nice."

"Hey, *you* laughed when I said it," Paul pointed out.

"True."

"And I didn't even tell you that my grandfather's name is Fritz."

Holly laughed. "No way."

"Way. Which is why he thinks it's so hilarious to say 'on the fritz.'"

"Is this the grandfather whose sense of humor you inherited?" Holly teased. Finally they were getting along the way he and Ainslee seemed to.

"Hold on a second. Are there any pickles in the fridge?" Paul called from the pantry.

Holly dried her hands and opened the refrigerator door. "Nope. I don't see any."

"Then we're out of pickles," he said as he walked out of the pantry. "We're totally out of them."

"We are? Really?"

"I told you you were using too many. There's no jars left," Paul complained.

"I didn't use too many," Holly protested. She remembered Paul staring at her as she loaded a grilled cheese with a layer of pickles the day before.

"You did."

"Anyway, so I was trying to make the sandwiches more flavorful. Sue me."

"You practically ate them all yourself on that sandwich you made yesterday. So what are we going to do today for your so-called flavor?" Paul demanded.

"Salt?" Holly suggested.

"Seriously." Paul glared at her.

"Wow." Holly took a step back. "You're really concerned. You know, people lived without pickles for, like, aeons and aeons."

"Yeah. And this kitchen ran smoothly for, like, aeons. Until you got here," Paul said.

Did he wake up on the wrong side of the bed or something? Holly wondered. "That's not what Russell said. He said last summer was the nightmare," she said in self-defense.

"Okay, but being out of pickles? It's what Russell would call a problem," Paul said.

"Fine. Problems need solutions," Holly quoted Russell. "Okay, so. Can the food service place bring more pickles today?"

Paul shook his head. "No, we only get deliveries two days a week. You know that. You know, this is all your fault."

Holly turned to him. "Fine. How many times do you need to say that?"

Paul shrugged. "A couple more."

"We could put up a sign. We're out of pickles,"

Holly said. "I'll draw a funny picture. Nobody will care."

"There's that tennis tournament today. We'll be mobbed. People will want burgers," Paul said.

Holly had to smile, thinking about how Paul had evaluated everyone's orders ahead of time. "Can't we serve burgers without pickles?"

"I guess. But we can't be out of stuff because it looks bad," Paul said. "I mean, what if Mrs. Whittingham, who always orders extra pickles on her sandwiches, comes by, and we have this lame sign up about no pickles?"

"It wouldn't be a lame sign," Holly muttered. "I can draw. But okay, I get your point." This wasn't her fault, but if she could fix the problem, then she and Paul could get back to working in whatever small amount of harmony they'd started to have. She definitely didn't want to stand there and listen to him go on and on about everything being her fault. Not in the middle of a heat wave.

"You know what? You can do all this prep stuff by yourself, right?" she asked him.

He shrugged. "Sure."

"Then I'll go to the store. I'll be back as soon as I can, okay?"

"I — I guess so," Paul stammered, looking confused. "But how are you going to . . . do you have a car?"

"Don't worry about it. I'll ask someone in the office to take me." Holly grabbed her wallet and rushed out the door.

"You did what?"

Paul just stood there, holding the heavy white plastic grocery bags, which were filled with glass jars of pickles.

Holly brushed her hair out of her eyes. She really hated having helmet hair on the hottest day of the year, when the A/C wasn't working. "I rode to the Food Value."

"Rode. On your bike," Paul said. "Food Value? That's like ten miles away. And it's really, really hot out."

"Actually, it feels hotter in here," Holly said. "At least outside there's a breeze."

"Hold on. Let me get you something to drink." Paul set the bags on the counter. He grabbed a large cup and filled it with ice and soda.

"Please, no Retro-ade," Holly said.

"No, of course not." He handed her the giant

cup. Then, as she gulped soda, he took out a few of the pickle jars and examined them.

"I got a couple different kinds," Holly said.

"Of course you did. That's you," said Paul.

"Variety girl. But not garden-variety girl," Holly murmured. "Mrs. Whittingham has this big garden. We should go there. Too bad it's in England." She could hear Paul running water in the background.

"I think you're a little light-headed. Here. Put this around your neck." He gave her a wet dish towel. "Just sit for a second. Don't talk."

"Why not?"

"Because you're not making sense. Hold on, I can get you a fresh T-shirt. Might be a little big, but you can handle that for one day, right?"

He pulled out of his duffel a faded red T-shirt that said SOUTHWEST SOCCER on it.

Holly had always totally envied her sisters when they wore their boyfriends' hoodies or sweaters. She couldn't believe Paul was giving her his shirt.

"It's clean," Paul insisted when she hesitated.

"Oh, no — it wasn't that. I was just thinking." *Thinking that this is kind of ultrapersonal.* Like, how many guys had ever given her their shirt before?

"Thinking?" Paul prompted.

"You know those giant walk-in freezers and coolers? Wouldn't it be nice if we had one of those?" *And we could get locked in or something. And it would be really romantic until the part where we started shivering and then froze to death.*

"Go change," Paul insisted.

"Okay, I will." She couldn't believe how nice he was being.

"Wow. You seriously rode all the way to Food Value for me?" Paul asked.

"No. For pickles," she said. "Someone's waiting." She pointed to a couple standing at the counter, then slipped out to the locker room to change her shirt.

She pulled the Southwest Soccer tee over her head, then brushed and tied her hair back. She looked at her reflection in the mirror. She hoped none of her teammates would come into the club and see her in their rival school's T-shirt.

Then again — what was she even thinking? Hopefully they would come by. This was Paul West's shirt she was wearing. Soccer star. Arrogant jerk.

Except for when he was being nice and handing out shirts.

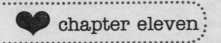

chapter eleven

"I can't believe the A/C isn't fixed yet," Paul said. "I mean, how long are we supposed to stand here?"

"And I can't believe anyone actually wants to eat anything." Holly hadn't had an appetite the last few days, thanks to the heat wave.

"Yeah, well, it's not like they're hanging around after they get their food. They sit outside. At least there's a breeze out there."

"What are you talking about? We have a breeze." They'd turned on a giant fan that was blowing straight into their faces.

"More like a tropical wind," Paul said.

"We should have worn Hawaiian shirts or something. That reminds me — I have your shirt. Remind me to give it to you before we leave tonight."

"Give my shirt to me before we leave," Paul

said. "There, I just reminded you." When Holly frowned at him, he said, "You said to remind you. You didn't say when."

"Okay, could you not be so obnoxious when the heat is, like, a thousand degrees in here?" Holly stood at the grill, cooking four hot dogs and one veggie burger.

"Hot dogs still outsell veggies," Paul commented as he watched her.

"It's four kids and one mom," she told him. "Kids are cheap, anyway." Holly felt a trickle of sweat roll down from behind her neck, under her hair, all the way down her back. She jumped as the bad burner flared up. "Great. All we need is more fire in here."

About five minutes later, she was looking at the so-called "climate control" thermometer when Paul came up beside her. "What are you doing?"

"Checking the temp in here. I feel like I'm going to pass out. This is worse than the day I rode to Food Value."

"You mean . . . yesterday? You want some ice water?"

"I've had about a gallon," Holly said.

"So what does it say?" Paul asked. He leaned closer to look over her shoulder.

It says warm verging on too warm, Holly thought. She felt as if she was about to melt. Not in a sultry way, either. More like a piece of American cheese on a hamburger.

"It says, uh, hot. Extremely hot," Holly said, feeling a little weak in the knees. "Ninety-two? You know, you might not want to stand so close. If I pass out, I'll take you down with me." *Of course, that wasn't a* bad *image*, she thought with a smile.

Paul stepped back, giving her a little room. "I wish we had one of those walk-in freezers. We could go inside and hang out."

Holly smiled uneasily, remembering her same thought the day before about getting trapped in one with Paul. "No doubt."

"You know what we should do? We should both call in sick. Take the whole day off tomorrow," Paul said.

"We should?" What exactly was he asking her, anyway? To spend a day off with him?

"Yes. In protest. I mean, do they really expect us to work under these conditions?"

"You sound like you're ready to go on strike," Holly commented.

"That's it. Strike!" Paul shouted, pumping his fist in the air.

Russell's face suddenly appeared at the window. "Is there a problem?" Russell asked.

"Well, *yeah*, Russell, there is," Paul said.

"I thought I heard the word *strike*. Did I?" Russell looked petrified. His star employee appeared to be falling apart right in front of him. "What's wrong, Paul?"

"Haven't you noticed? That we look like we're about to keel over?" Paul said.

"You don't look exactly, uh, fresh, no," Russell agreed.

"We have been broiling in here for two days straight, because of the broken air-conditioning," Paul said. "Maybe it doesn't affect other people so much because they're not working in boiling-hot kitchens, but we want to know — is there anything being done to fix it? At all?"

Russell just stared at the two of them. He looked like he was about to yell. Finally he said, "Get out of here, you two. Hit the pool."

"What?"

"You're kidding."

Russell shook his head. "Nope. You've got half an hour. Shoo. They're fixing the A/C now and it should be up and running soon, so I'll hang around until it is, and —"

Russell was still talking when Holly and Paul took off for the locker rooms to change.

"Last one in is a rotten egg!" Paul called.

"Not fair!" Holly shouted as she sprinted into the women's locker room. Did he have any idea how long it took to put on a bathing suit with two halves?

Holly and Paul came out of the locker rooms at almost exactly the same time.

They both stood facing the pool instead of each other.

And then they started laughing.

The pool was full of a group of older adults. Much older. Holly looked out at a sea of floral white, pink, fuchsia, and lime-green bathing caps.

A sign beside the pool said:

3 P.M. GERIATRI-CIZE CLASS. SWIMMIN' TO THE OLDIES!

Paul and Holly looked at each other. "What should we do?" Paul said.

"I thought we were going to go swimming," Holly said. "So what's stopping you?"

"Yeah, but, can we when there's a class going on?" Paul asked.

"Russell said we could. He sort of almost ordered us to hit the pool, if you look at it that way. And it's almost four o'clock, so the class is almost over. And I know I need to geriatri-cize a *lot* more often."

Paul started laughing. "Yeah. Well, it's swimming to the oldies. And I'm old," Paul said.

"How old?" Holly asked. This was something she'd wanted to know, but had been too chicken to ask before.

"Seventeen. You?"

"Fifteen," Holly said. "But only for a couple more days," she quickly added.

Paul shrugged. "Then we're qualified. Come on."

And he dove into the pool. Before she could lose her nerve, Holly followed him and plunged into the cool, refreshing water. She surfaced right next to Paul. "Wow. This feels so good," she said.

"Yeah." He glanced over at her as they both treaded water. "Rotten egg."

"Am not," Holly said.

"You were last one in. Even your great grand-mother over there got in before you," he teased.

Holly flicked water in his face. "Shut up. As if you're so brave. I had to talk you into even diving in."

"I was trying to respect my elders," Paul said, then he dove underwater again. Paul kept coming to the surface and then going underneath again. Holly floated on her back, relaxing and letting the motion of the pool gently rock her body.

Holly and Paul stayed in the deep end of the pool, near the diving board. The adults weren't exercising down that way, because they couldn't touch bottom.

One of the purple plastic beach balls the class was using to exercise with drifted down to the deep end.

Holly and Paul started fighting over it, trying to kick it like a soccer ball. "Ever play water polo?" Paul asked.

"Nope," Holly replied.

"Come on, try it. It's like soccer, but you have to swim all the time and use your arms instead of your lcgs."

"So . . . how is that like soccer?" Holly asked, smoothing her hair back from her face. "In any way?"

"Shut up." He swam over and tried to dunk her head underwater.

"Don't —" She fought back, and they ended up wrestling each other, fighting for the beach ball.

"Hey, that —"

"Watch it —"

"Give it to me —"

And both of them were laughing hysterically as they went underwater, surfaced, and went under again. As they came back above water, arms tangled together, they looked at each other and were like: *What are we doing? We don't do this.*

"Quit it," Holly said, swimming away a little bit.

"I wasn't doing anything," Paul said. They were both panting and out of breath. "I just have one thing to say."

"What's that?" asked Holly.

"Swim much?"

"You are so dead!" She pushed off the wall with her feet and plowed into Paul, submerging him as far as she could. When they were both underwater, he grabbed her foot.

"Stop! That tickles!" she shouted underwater,

in a flurry of bubbles. She kicked out, trying to get away from him.

He let go of her foot, and Holly swam to the surface. Seconds later, Paul surfaced, too. He was holding his nose and looked like he was in pain. "Maybe you should play offense instead of goal. You have a serious kick," Paul said. He wouldn't take his hand away from his nose. "You could score lots of goals."

"I'm really sorry. Does it hurt?" Holly quickly swam over to him.

"Oh, no. Only when I *breathe*," he complained.

"Oh my God. I'm so sorry! Let me see," Holly urged. They were standing almost in the middle of the pool, so the water came up to their shoulders. "No, come on, let me see." She slowly peeled back his fingers from his nose. She found herself standing closer to Paul than she realized at first.

"Do you, um, think I broke it?" Holly asked.

"No. It's fine," Paul said, smiling at her. "I was maybe exaggerating a little."

"Oh." Suddenly Holly found it a little hard to breathe. She got that feeling again as she and Paul looked at each other. *Is something happening?*

Then a shower of water rained down on

Holly's head. She turned to see Ainslee standing on the edge of the pool in her bikini, kicking water at them.

"What are you guys doing?" Ainslee cried, hands on her hips. "You're supposed to *tell* me when it's pool party time." She dove in and swam over to them.

Holly was usually thrilled to see her best friend show up — anywhere, anytime. But right now, she sort of wished she hadn't.

"So. What did I miss?" Ainslee asked.

"Holly tried to break my nose," Paul said.

"Holly!" Ainslee shoved her playfully. "She's a crazy swimmer, but don't worry. I'll protect you," she told Paul.

chapter twelve

"Good afternoon is the manager here thank you."

A man wearing a blue shirt and tie talked so quickly that Holly wasn't quite sure she'd heard him correctly. "I'm sorry — did you say the manager?" she asked.

"Yes. My name is Hector. I am the health inspector. We have an unscheduled appointment to come by and investigate," he said.

Holly glanced up at the clock. It was almost four-thirty. "How can it be an appointment if it's not scheduled?" Holly wondered out loud.

Hector didn't look like he wanted to get into a discussion with her. About anything. "The manager. Are you the manager?" he repeated.

"No, sir. His name is Russell, but he's not here right now," she said.

"Well, who else is here?" he demanded.

"This is Paul." Holly coughed. "Paul West.

139

He's the senior employee around here, so maybe he could help you."

"I'm the what?" Paul asked as he walked up. "Did you just call me the boss? Cool."

"I'm here to do your annual health inspection," Hector said.

"Me?" Paul asked, looking aghast.

"No. The establishment. May I come in?" Hector asked.

"Oh, right. Of course. Sure!" Holly hurried over to unlock the door beside the walk-up window.

Hector rapidly listed off all the areas and items he'd be inspecting, then told them to get back to work as they normally would.

"Good thing he's here today instead of when the A/C was broken," Paul whispered to Holly, as Hector took out a thermometer.

He seemed to be checking the cleanliness of the counters, the pantry, and the stove. He tested the temperature of food, both cold and hot.

"Is there anything you need to tell me about the kitchen?" Hector asked as he checked out the oven.

"You know, there's this burner —" Holly began.

Paul pinched her in the ribs. She let out a little squeak, and he held her there for a second.

Hector tapped his pen against his clipboard. "Did you say something about a burner? Is it a malfunction?"

"Who, me? Oh, no." Embarrassed, Holly stepped away from Paul. "I was just saying I got, uh, a sunburn, because it was a real sunburner yesterday. That's what we call them around here. Sunburners."

"Overkill," Paul coughed.

Hector stood up and stared at her. "I don't see —"

"It's on my stomach. If you want to see —"

Hector's ears turned bright red, and he stared at the floor. "No, that's fine."

"Are you sure? It's really bad. It's killing me."

"I'll take a look," Paul offered. "Put some lotion on there for you."

Holly jabbed him with her elbow. "Anyway. I can't think of any problems around here, can you?" she asked, turning to Paul.

He shrugged. "Nope."

"Actually, it's not up to you to declare problems," Hector said. "It's for me to discover them. Now, if you don't mind, and quite frankly even if you do, I'd like to inspect the refrigerator."

"No problem." Paul gave Holly a superior

smile. He always insisted on cleaning the fridge at the end of every afternoon.

It was like he knew this day was coming, thought Holly. Wait a second. Maybe he did. After all, he hadn't seemed surprised. Also, he'd been here last year.

Paul pulled at the sleeve of Holly's T-shirt, urging her over toward the counter. He picked up an order pad and quickly jotted down, *Hector the Health Inspector? Is that a new reality show?*

No. It's an old, bad movie, she wrote back.

She couldn't remember the last time she'd passed notes back and forth. Sixth grade, maybe?

"Do you have something you want to tell me?" Hector asked.

"No, sir," Paul said quickly.

"Are you sure?"

"Very," Paul replied. "We were just going over the new menu. Want to make sure we get it all right."

While Hector continued to poke around the kitchen, Holly looked out and spotted an older woman dressed in a completely argyle golf outfit coming their way. There was no mistaking her.

"Paul. Paul," Holly said, nudging him in the

ribs — or trying to, but hitting his hip instead because he was too tall. "Mrs. Whittingham's coming! What else is going to go wrong today?"

"Relax. Nothing's going wrong," Paul said. "We'll handle it."

"Hello there — a new Bannon, wasn't it?" Mrs. Whittingham asked, and Holly wished that for once she was wearing her name tag. "And Paul, a pleasure as always."

"Oh, the pleasure's all mine," Paul replied politely.

"Ours," Holly added.

Mrs. Whittingham rapped her knuckles against the wood counter. "I've heard about this new menu from Russell. Let's see it!"

"Right there, Mrs. Whittingham," Holly said, showing her the blackboard with colored chalk listings.

Hector peered around the corner, as if he wanted to inspect the chalkboard menu for germs as well.

"I'm the owner of this club, and I don't remember seeing you around here before," Mrs. Whittingham said to Hector. "Who are you?"

"I'm the health inspector," he said.

"I'm sure everything has passed with flying colors," Mrs. Whittingham said, making it sound as if the issue wasn't up for debate.

"Well, yes," Hector said, sounding disappointed. "Everything checked out just fine."

"Wonderful. Why don't you have a club sandwich with me, they're excellent," Mrs. Whittingham said.

"I can't eat on the job. But thank you, anyway." Hector nodded to her, then slapped a pink copy of their report on the counter and took off.

"Strange little man," Mrs. Whittingham commented. "I'll be over there — bring me an Arnold Palmer with the club, won't you? Oh, and extra pickles, of course." She headed to an empty table.

"Yes, ma'am. Be right there!" Paul promised her. He turned to Holly. "Did you hear that? Extra pickles. Just like I told you."

Holly smiled at Paul. "Yeah, and thanks to me, we have plenty," she said.

"Pickles aren't everything," Paul muttered as he grabbed the lettuce and tomato from the fridge.

"No, they're the *only* thing. And if you say I have weird taste again, just remember that I share it with her. Why don't we have a ham-and-cheese sandwich on the menu?" Holly asked as she stood at the toaster preparing the bread for Mrs. Whittingham's club sandwich. "We could call it Mrs. Whitting-ham-and-cheese?"

"Okay. *No*," Paul laughed. "Not ever."

"What a day," Holly sighed.

"Okay, so, we scored on impressing the boss," Paul said as he faced the empty patio. They were closing up for the night, pulling down the canvas screen.

"And not only did we pass the health inspection, we passed it with flying colors in *front* of the boss," Holly said. "We should get a raise or something."

"Right. Or an extra vacation day."

"Extra? Do we get any?" Holly asked.

"No, I guess not. Hey, maybe we should have ice cream, to celebrate," Paul said. "We passed the health inspection. We impressed Mrs. W. with our new menu —"

"*Our* new menu?" Holly repeated, shoving his arm. "Uh-huh."

"I could really go for a banana split," Paul said. "In one of those chocolate-coated waffle cones at Dairy Creme."

Holly's mouth watered, just thinking about it. "Yeah. Me too."

"You have your bike here, right?" Paul asked. "So do I. We could ride to the Dairy Creme."

Holly thought about it for a second. Was he kind of, sort of, asking her out? And why did that make her panic? "You know, that's a good idea. Let me run over to the courts and ask Ainslee if she wants to come along." After all, Ainslee was the one who was *really* interested in Paul. She had to think of her first.

"Why would we ask Ainslee?"

"Because she'd, um, want to know. She's manic about ice cream," Holly said. "And if I go over there and ask Ainslee I should probably ask Ross, too, because it'd be rude not to."

"Ross, too?" Paul stood there for a second, just looking at her.

"What?" She laughed, feeling uncomfortable.

"Does he have to come?" Paul asked.

"No, he doesn't have to," Holly said. "He might not even be able to, because he might be busy —"

"You know what? Forget it. I just remembered something I have to do." Paul picked up his duffel. "I'd better take off. See you tomorrow."

146

What did I do wrong? Holly wondered as he headed out the door and down the hall. *Everything was going fine, until I mentioned Ainslee and Ross. What does he have against them?*

Suddenly Holly remembered something. She dashed out into the hallway after him. "Wait — Paul! Wait up!"

He turned around and gave her a big smile. "Yeah?" He jogged back toward her.

"I totally forgot the other day, even though you were supposed to remind me." She handed him a plastic bag. "Here's your T-shirt. I washed it, so it's totally clean. No Holly germs left."

"Great. That's just great," Paul mumbled as he stuffed the shirt into his duffel.

"Um . . . is everything okay?" Holly asked. "Are you mad at me or something?"

Paul shook his head. "No, I was just — wondering when you were going to return it. That's exactly what I wanted. I was wondering what took so long."

"Oh. Sorry! I kept forgetting it. Thanks again. You totally saved the day when you gave me that," Holly told him.

"Yeah. Well, you really smelled," Paul replied.

"Shut up, I did not," Holly said.

"So it was more like I was saving the rest of us." He turned and started jogging over to the bike rack.

"Yeah, good-bye to you, too!" Holly called after him.

"And your dumb shirt, which I wouldn't want to be caught dead in, actually," she added under her breath.

chapter thirteen

"So what did your parents do for your birthday?" Ainslee asked as they walked into the club a few days later.

"My dad made blueberry pancakes," Holly said. "Then they gave me a key to the old Subaru."

"You're kidding! You're getting a *car*?" Ainslee cried.

"Not exactly. What Mom said was that I could have it when I turn seventeen," Holly explained. "So the gift is that this year I get my license, and if I don't have any 'major mishaps,' which is how they put it, then next year I can have the car. By which time it'll be completely broken down, because my sisters drove it into the ground, but oh well."

"Hey, who cares. It's a car," Ainslee commented. "That means we'll have one senior year!"

"Sure, Ains, *we* will," Holly said.

"So. Any other gifts yet?"

"Just a few little things from my sisters," Holly said. "Earrings, a journal — cool stuff, actually."

"My mom says you always find out how people really feel about you on your birthday," Ainslee said. "Like, people you hardly know will come out of the woodwork and spring for these nice gifts. And people you consider your friends will give you these crappy re-gifts."

"Well, *that* sounds like a great birthday." Holly laughed. "Wait. Are you planning to re-gift me?"

"No, I'd never," Ainslee said. "I just think it's interesting, that's all." They stopped outside the open door to the club kitchen. "Hey, Paul!" she called.

Paul was sitting on the counter with his back to the patio, and he looked up from the magazine he was reading. "Yeah?" he asked.

"It's Holly's birthday," Ainslee said.

"Yeah, I knew it was her birthday; you told me a couple of days ago." He went back to reading.

"Um . . . 'happy birthday' would kind of be the normal response?" Ainslee said.

He kept reading for a second. Then he looked up and sighed, "Happy birthday," and went back to reading.

"What were you saying about finding out how

people really feel about you on your birthday?" Holly whispered.

"It's going to be a fun day — forget about him," Ainslee said. "Happy birthday!" she shouted over her shoulder as she dashed off toward the tennis courts.

Holly walked into the kitchen and worked around Paul to get things ready. She didn't say anything, and he didn't, either. As the morning went on, whenever they bumped into each other, she felt really awkward.

"Excuse me," she said as she reached past him.

"No, excuse me," he said.

Whenever anyone came to the counter to order, Paul talked to them just like he normally would. They got through the early lunch rush without talking, just taking orders and filling them individually. When they absolutely had to talk, they did — but that was it.

So this is what it's like when Paul's mad at you, Holly thought. But she didn't know what to say. If she apologized, what would she be apologizing for? What if Paul was in a bad mood about something that had nothing to do with her?

The summer wasn't even quite half over. If she

really embarrassed herself with Paul now, she wouldn't be able to keep working there without constant daily reminders of how she'd thought he was interested — when he wasn't. But she had to say *some*thing.

Holly cleared her throat as she filled a soda cup for herself. She took a sip and looked over at him. "So, uh —"

"I'm going to take my break now," Paul said, and he was out the door before she could even ask "What?" or "How long?"

Russell strolled into the kitchen at about three o'clock. "Hey, guys. Any problems?"

Holly glanced at Paul. "No, no problems." *Unless you consider the fact that Paul doesn't speak to me anymore.*

"Good, I can't deal with any problems." Russell grabbed an apron from the closet and slipped it over his head. "Holly, you get to leave early today. Happy birthday!"

"Seriously?" asked Holly. Because she wouldn't mind getting out of there for a while. The silent treatment was killing her.

Russell handed her a birthday card. "Seriously.

Your friend Ainslee said to meet her over at court two, so you can take off together."

"Are you sure?" Holly asked.

Russell nodded. "Paul and I can hold down the fort."

Why did she get the feeling she was being pushed out? Like Paul had asked specifically to *not* work with her?

Holly spent a few minutes getting cleaned up, then she headed outside. She left her bag in the kitchen, to force herself to come back later and maybe try to talk to Paul again. Not that he'd talk *back*.

When she got to the courts to meet Ainslee, she saw a clump of people gathered there. *Tournament time*, she thought. Hopefully she wouldn't be forced to play tennis on her birthday.

"Here she comes!" she heard someone yell.

And then everyone turned around and cried, "Happy birthday, Holly!"

There was a big paper banner strung along the tennis net that said HAPPY SWEAT SIXTEEN!

"I didn't sweat sixteen as much as I sweated seventeen," Toby joked, standing beside Holly.

"What?" asked Ainslee. She checked out the

banner. "Ross! It's supposed to say *sweet*, not *sweat*!" she cried.

"Spell-check," he said with a shrug. "Sorry."

"Do you not proofread?" Ainslee jogged over with a pen and started trying to turn the *A* in *sweat* into an *E*.

"It's kind of appropriate, actually," said Holly. "This summer's been pretty hot."

"No doubt," Toby agreed. "Hey, where's Paul?"

Holly shrugged. *Not here. Because he hates me. Because he doesn't care that it's my birthday.* "Still working, I guess," she said.

"Seriously?" Toby said.

Holly nodded. "Seriously."

"Everyone, help yourselves to cupcakes before they melt!" Ainslee pointed to a folding card table. "They're in the serving box. Get it?"

"Tennis humor. Hilarious," Toby commented with a frown, and then walked away from them.

Ross came over to Holly and handed her a birthday card. Inside, he'd written that the card was good for one free tennis lesson.

"But, Ross. I already get free lessons," Holly said.

"Yeah. I know." He laughed. "It was the only

thing I could think of. You can wait until after the summer and redeem it or something."

"Sure. Sounds great. Thanks," Holly said.

Ainslee turned to Holly. "I forgot the cups for the punch. Be right back."

"See what I mean? She never talks to me," Ross said as they watched Ainslee disappear into the building.

Ross and Holly made small talk for a minute or two, until Holly noticed Paul walking out onto the tennis court. Actually, he wasn't walking. Ainslee was sort of dragging him by the arm.

If he was coming to the party for her, maybe it wasn't completely hopeless. She started heading in his direction when a group of other employees stepped in front of her.

"Happy birthday!" they cried.

"Hey, guys. Thanks for coming!" Holly said, as they broke into a loud, off-tune verse of "Happy Birthday."

She thanked them, then ran into a few other friends, then searched for Paul again. Aha! There he was, with Toby, trying to play hackysack with a tennis ball. Well, this would be embarrassing, but she had no choice.

She walked toward them, but before she got there Mrs. Whittingham walked onto the tennis court, wearing golfing clothes, her golf shoe spikes clattering on the playing surface. "What's going on here?"

A caddy followed her, carrying her bag of golf clubs, and behind her stood her assistant, carrying a large coffee mug for her.

Holly panicked for a second. Had Ainslee gotten permission to *do* all this?

"I heard there was a birthday party. Now, who's the birthday girl or boy, and where's the cake?"

Ainslee stepped up with the plate of cupcakes she'd brought from home, while Mrs. Whittingham congratulated Holly. They spoke for a few minutes, then she turned around and looked for Paul.

Everyone around Holly was talking and laughing, but she could hardly focus on what they were saying. It didn't matter.

She didn't know that finding someone to like would feel like this. And it was great and it was horrible. It was like she couldn't even have a good time at her own birthday party unless he talked to her.

She sat down on the bench beside the court and sipped her punch. She should really go home, she thought. The party was winding down, and she was looking pathetic.

"Hey, happy birthday." Paul sat down on the bench beside her.

Holly felt her heart leap. *This is it,* she thought. *Here's my chance.* "Hey — thanks. I was looking for you."

"Yeah?"

Ask him, Holly. Ask him if he wants to go out, or something. Anything.

But she couldn't.

"Well, anyway. Here," Paul said. He handed her a small white plastic bag.

"This better not be a present," Holly told him.

"Why not?"

"Because! You shouldn't have —"

"It's not much, okay? Don't freak."

"I wasn't," Holly said. "Was I?"

She reached into the bag and pulled out a pair of soft white athletic socks. They had three red stripes around the top.

"They're really good socks. They, uh, don't fall down," Paul explained.

"Thanks! Wow, what a great gift," she said.

"Anyway, I should get back — Russell will panic if I don't," Paul said. "See you tomorrow."

"But, um, Paul?" Holly asked as he got to his feet.

"Yeah?"

"Have a cupcake before you go," Holly said.

He gave her a strange look and she sank down on the bench, utterly disgusted with herself. Why was it so impossible to know what to say to him?

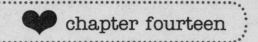

chapter fourteen

"Will this club never stop with its social events?" Holly stood outside the club's front doors the next morning, staring at a giant bright neon sign taped to the wall.

"Midsummer Night's Dream," Ainslee read out loud. "Party at Ridgemont — guests and staff both invited!"

Holly lazily rubbed her eyes. She hadn't been able to sleep. She really wanted to see Paul and thank him for the socks, which she'd worn to bed even though it was the middle of summer (which she wouldn't tell him).

Then she hadn't been able to sleep because she couldn't stop thinking about him (which she also wouldn't tell him) and wondering if maybe they really did have chemistry and should be going out (which she wouldn't tell him or Ainslee).

"Really. It's kind of ridiculous," Ainslee agreed, "and it also sounds incredibly dorky."

"Yes," said Holly. "It does. It's all Shakespearean and old-fashioned. Like the Ridgemont Country Club itself."

Ainslee smiled. "Which is exactly why it makes sense, I guess. And you know what else? It does give us options."

"Options," Holly repeated.

"Excuses, more like. We can ask the guys we've been wanting to ask out — we have an excuse. I mean, if we have to . . . and it's a club activity . . ."

"What are you saying?"

"Summer is disappearing already and we still have to find dates. For real," Ainslee declared. "So? What do you think? It's been a while since we talked about this. Are you still hating Paul or are you thinking he's Extremely Cute Guy again?"

"I don't know," Holly said.

"How can you not know?"

Holly wasn't sure she could explain it. She was somewhere between the two.

"I thought you pretty much didn't get along, despite that chemistry. Because chemistry is important, but it's not everything," Ainslee proclaimed.

Holly raised her eyebrow. "Let me guess. Your mom."

Ainslee shrugged. "The woman talks a lot. Which is très embarrassing most of the time. Anyway, you know I think Paul's cute, but you did pick him out first. So go ahead. Ask him today."

"T-today?" Holly stammered. "You mean, like, right now?"

"Why wait?" Ainslee asked. "And if you decide not to, then I will. No pressure."

"Right, not much," Holly muttered as Ainslee skipped off to the tennis courts.

"Good luck!" she called over her shoulder.

Why wait? Because I don't want to get rejected. Because I don't want to sound stupid. Because I've never asked anyone out before!

No pressure.

This was the complete opposite of "no pressure."

Holly stood in the kitchen doorway, a dozen different approaches running through her mind. Then she saw a figure walk out of the pantry.

"Russell?" she asked. "Where's Paul?"

"He called in sick. You're stuck with me today." Russell dropped a giant can of Retro-ade on the counter. "I can't believe we still haven't used all this up."

161

Holly heaved a sigh of relief. "Paul's sick. Good."

Russell looked at her. "You're . . . glad he's sick?"

"No, of course not — I just — sorry, I was thinking of something else." *Like: Now I don't have to ask him. Thank goodness. Or not, because maybe I did want to ask him.*

And: Is he really sick, or is he just avoiding me?

That night Holly sat on her bed, in her room, staring at the phone. She had to call Paul. Now. She'd set the timer on her cell phone, giving her five minutes to prepare. The alarm had gone off ten minutes ago.

All she could think about was what Ainslee had said: "Why wait? And if you decide not to, then I will. No pressure."

Holly was starting to get a splitting headache from all the lack of pressure.

A dozen different openings went through her mind. None of them any good.

"Hi, Paul. Yes, it's me. Holly. *Holly?* Your coworker?" She paused for a second. "Holly Bannon. Bethany's sister?"

She coughed, then started over. "Paul, are you okay? Are you really sick? Are you avoiding me?"

No, that wouldn't do. She'd have to be more subtle than that.

But if she was too subtle, he wouldn't figure out what she was calling about.

Holly cleared her throat. "Yes, hello, this is Holly Bannon calling," she practiced. "Is Paul there by any chance?" she asked in as sultry a voice as she could muster.

Why would she try to be sultry to someone else who answered the phone? This was all wrong.

"Hey. Paul. It's me." That was all she really wanted to say. "I'm sorry about the pickles incident, and about kicking you in the face that one day in the pool. Will you go out with me?"

All of a sudden her phone rang, completely startling her. It was Ainslee's ring tone, so she grabbed it and said, "Hey."

"Hey. What are you doing?" Ainslee asked.

"Oh, ah, nothing much." There were some things it was too embarrassing to even tell your best friend in the entire world, even when you told her everything else.

"Me either," Ainslee said. "I have a question for you. Did you ask Paul yet?"

"No," Holly said. "He called in sick today, remember?"

"Well, yeah, but we've been home for a while, so you could call him," Ainslee said.

"Right. But what if he's, you know, really sick?" Holly said. "He needs his rest and he shouldn't be up late talking on the phone. He probably has a really bad headache, too." *Like the one I'm getting*, thought Holly. *From making up all these lame excuses*.

"Holly? Are you afraid to ask him or something?" asked Ainslee.

Holly sighed. "Okay, fine, I'm procrastinating."

"Well, what's the deal? Because don't kill me, but I was talking to my mom, and she said that sometimes if you wait too long, then it can ruin a relationship."

"We don't have a relationship," Holly said.

"Okay, so that's what I wanted to ask. I mean, I totally don't want to step on your toes. Like I said before, you were the one who picked out Paul that first night. But do you think it's going anywhere with you and Paul?" Ainslee asked.

"Um." Holly thought about all the things that had happened between them. Getting caught in the rain together. Jumping into the pool. Being busted by Hector the Health Inspector.

And then she thought of how cold he'd been to her on her birthday. But then he'd given her a gift. But then he'd called in sick, which he'd never done before, according to Russell.

"Not really, I guess," she said.

"Because maybe the fact you can't call him means that you're not supposed to be together. You know?" asked Ainslee.

Or, maybe it means I'm a chicken, Holly thought. "Right," she said.

"Okay, well . . . is it okay if *I* ask him to that dance, then?"

Holly had known that Ainslee was planning to do this. So why did she feel like the wind had been completely knocked out of her? It reminded her of a soccer game when she'd collided with another player and fallen to the ground. In a heap. She was so stunned she couldn't say anything then, or now.

"Well," she finally squeaked. "I guess."

"So you don't care if I ask him out?"

Do I care? Holly thought. *Do I care that the guy who I can't stop thinking about, who I'm totally into, who drives me crazy, might go out with you?*

"Oh, no. It's cool," she said.

Fortunately this was over the phone, so Ainslee couldn't see the tortured expression on Holly's face. If she had, she would never have gone on and on about how cool she thought Paul was and how they always had such great conversations and how he was such a good athlete.

Obviously he and Ainslee had hit it off.

And he and Holly hadn't.

Take her birthday party — she hadn't even managed to talk to him, except that one awkward time. And instead of saying something meaningful, or trying to ask him out, she hadn't said anything much except "have a cupcake."

She wasn't cut out for this summer fling thing. This wasn't the way it was supposed to work. It was all supposed to be light and fun and natural.

But it wasn't.

Ainslee's mom was right: If something was going to happen between her and Paul, it would have already happened. They'd had tons of opportunities. Obviously, it wasn't meant to be.

"So, is it really all right if I call him?" asked Ainslee.

"How many times are you going to ask me?

Sure," Holly said. "And, uh, good luck!" It seemed like the only polite thing to say.

"I'll call you later," Ainslee promised. "Let you know how it goes. Then we can work on a list of people *you* can call."

"Great." Holly sighed and collapsed back on her bed for a couple of minutes, staring at the ceiling fan revolving above her. Why had she let everything turn into such a mess? What good was having four sisters and watching them go through all those dates and boyfriends if you didn't learn anything and were entirely clueless when it came time for you?

She remembered Bethany saying something once like, "When things don't work out, you just have to move on," and everyone else nodding in agreement.

If Ainslee was going to have a date for this thing, Holly needed a date, too.

The only guy she knew who might want to go with her was Ross. She ran her finger down the employee list, past B. Bannon (still wrong), and A. Smythe, down to . . .

P. WEST

Which came right before

R. WHITE

She felt kind of strange having the nerve to call Ross, when she couldn't bring herself to call Paul. What was that all about?

Ross answered right away, and seemed surprised to hear from her. Holly decided not to waste too much time on small talk. "I was wondering about this dance thing, at the club," she said. "Do you, uh, know about it?"

"Yeah, I read about it," Ross said. "I was kind of thinking of inviting Ainslee."

But you can't, thought Holly. *Because Ainslee's asking Paul, and I need to ask you to it!* Holly held the phone to her ear, feeling completely lost and unsure what to do next. Should she tell him that Ainslee was asking someone else? Should she tell him that she'd called to ask *him*?

"But what would be even cooler is if she actually asked me," Ross said. "You know?"

Don't hold your breath, Ross, Holly thought. "Right, it would be cool. But, uh . . ."

"Yeah, I know. I can't count on that. Actually this is kind of embarrassing. But I have to confess because I feel like I can tell you, because you already know. I've been sitting here for, like, an hour listening to Foo Fighters and trying to get up the nerve to call Ainslee. So I keep trying to think of how I can make it be about a Foo Fighters thing, like sort of casual. Then I'll spring it on her, about the party. What do you think?" asked Ross.

"I wouldn't, um, wait too long," Holly said. "That's what I think."

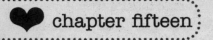

chapter fifteen

Ainslee's boyfriend.

That's how I'm going to have to start thinking of him. As Ainslee's boyfriend.

Why does that make me feel so ill? What's going on with me? It's just a fling we're talking about. A little summer romance. And if Ainslee found some-body, and I didn't, then oh well. Summer isn't over yet, is it?

Holly kept her eyes focused on the lettuce she was chopping, for two reasons:

(1) She didn't want to slice her fingers.

(2) Paul had just showed up for work and she didn't want Paul to think she wanted to talk, because if he did, he'd probably start telling her how happy he was that he worked with her, because he got to know Ainslee, and now they were madly in love, or something like that.

The whole thing made Holly feel so uncomfortable and upset that she hadn't even wanted to go to work with Ainslee that morning. She didn't want to hear how wonderfully it all went, how thrilled Paul was when she called, how the two of them would be going to the dance together.

To make things even worse, there had been a message from Paul on the answering machine when she got in, announcing, "Hey, this is Paul. I'm going to be a bit late."

Funny. Ainslee was late that day, too. Just as Holly was wondering how she was going to avoid her, Ainslee had called saying she would meet Holly at the club because she had to go in early for something, which Holly didn't buy.

No, she probably felt so badly about the Paul situation that she was hiding from Holly. And Paul was hiding, too.

Or maybe they weren't even thinking about her. No, they had probably already gone out, for coffee or breakfast — together. They couldn't wait for the dance.

Holly had read an article about this once. "Boyfriend Poaching." But Paul hadn't been her boyfriend, so that didn't count, and she was pretty sure the only things Ainslee had ever poached were some eggs.

Still. She couldn't imagine feeling more awkward.

"Hey."

"Oh. Hey!" Holly looked up from the stove, where she was cooking a grilled-cheese-and-tomato sandwich for herself. She'd imagined a quiet little breakfast on her own. Now Paul was here. Now . . . she'd have to hear about him and Ainslee. Well, at least they hadn't come in to see her together.

As she flipped the sandwich with a spatula, her stomach flipped over, too.

Paul came closer to her and peered into the pan. "That looks good."

"Um, want half?" Holly offered.

"Sure."

"You didn't have breakfast yet, either?" she asked.

"Hey, there's no rule about how many breakfasts you can have." Paul grabbed two plates and a knife. As Holly slid the sandwich onto one plate, he cut it in half.

She grabbed the bottle of Italian dressing

from the refrigerator. "Want any on your half?" she asked.

"You put salad dressing on your sandwiches?" Paul asked.

"It goes really well with the tomato."

"No pickles, though? Hmm. Let me try." He stood behind her while she opened the bottle.

She thought there was a shaker top, but instead, almost the entire bottle came squirting out — just as the problem burner flared up. The oil from the dressing hit the flame — and poof! It all happened so fast that Holly didn't have time to react, only to smash into Paul as she jumped back from the growing flames.

"You left the burner on!" Paul cried. He grabbed a broom and jabbed at the dial for the burner, to shut it off. He tossed dish towels at the fire, trying to smother it, but the counter was on fire now, too.

Holly grabbed the fire extinguisher, unclipped the safety, and fired foam all over the place. The smoke alarm was going off, and now a louder alarm sounded.

"Let's get out of here!" they both cried. Paul grabbed Holly's hand and pulled her away. They ran outside onto the patio and tried to catch their breath.

"I only have one thing to say," Paul said, between panting. "We're going to need new sandwiches."

They both started laughing.

"If this place goes up in flames, we are so busted. We're fried," Holly said, between laughs.

"You mean, *you* are. I didn't do anything!" Paul said.

"Oh, sure, you never do anything! It's all me, right?" Holly pushed him playfully.

"If you could have seen your face with that fire extinguisher." He laughed as he pointed out a blackened corner of her tee. "Nice look."

"Slightly charred chic. Wow." Holly blinked. "That's scary if you think about it."

"No, it would only be really scary if you were wearing my shirt," Paul said.

"Oh, give me a break — you have, like, ten of them," Holly said. She brushed her hair back from her forehead and felt a sticky clump of extinguisher foam.

"Do you think the fire's really out?" Paul asked.

"Who cares? We're okay. And no big problems. We don't —"

"Want any problems," Paul chimed in, and

together they repeated Russell's mantra. "I hate it when there are problems. I can't handle problems!"

They started laughing again.

Speaking of problems. She had to find a way to say this. "So. How did it go with Ainslee last night?" She thought she heard sirens in the distance, but maybe it was just her nerves. Her brain was buzzing from nervousness. "Are you and Ainslee going to that party?"

"What party?"

"You know," Holly said. "That midsummer night thing here."

"Oh, that. But you said something about me and Ainslee going." Paul waved his hand in front of her face. "Are you suffering from smoke inhalation or something? Me and Ainslee? Since when?"

"Since she called you last night to ask you!" Holly blurted. She couldn't hold it in any longer. The suspense was killing her, but not killing her softly. Killing her brutally.

"Ainslee never called me." Paul stared at her, with a look of confusion. "Why would Ainslee call *me*?"

"Oh, uh." Holly felt her face turning bright

pink. She felt terrible for letting Paul know Ainslee was interested. "I don't know, I mean, it was something she sort of, you know, mentioned. . . ." *And something I've been dwelling on ever since. And I haven't slept. But don't let that concern you.*

"Okay, but . . ." Paul coughed. "I, you know. Like you."

Holly held her breath. *Like me what?* she wanted to ask. *Or how? Or what do I mean, anyway?* She was so flustered she couldn't say anything. She just kept looking up at him.

"If I was going to that party with anyone, it would be you," Paul continued.

"It — it would?" Holly stammered. She felt like jumping up and down and yelling, but she'd already caused a fire — did she really need to make more of a scene than there already was?

"Yeah," Paul said.

Say something. Now! Holly commanded herself. *Before this limited-time offer runs out!* "Cool. Because I wanted to go with you, too," Holly said. "I was going to call you last night, but —"

"Wait a second. I still don't understand. Why would I go out with Ainslee?" Paul asked.

"Well. Uh." Holly was still having trouble

getting words out of her mouth. "Because she asked you first?"

Paul snapped Holly with one of the dish towels he'd used to try to smother the flames. "I wouldn't go out with anyone else, just because they asked first."

What was he saying? Did he really want to go with her? "You know, why isn't anyone else leaving the building?" Holly asked, peering around. "Can't they smell smoke? Or maybe it's not smoky anymore. But I think I hear sirens, don't you?"

"Quit trying to change the subject," Paul said. "About that stupid dance thing. I was thinking *you* were going to invite me."

"I was, but . . ."

"But what?"

"I couldn't! Every time I tried, something came up."

"Yeah. It's called being a coward."

"What?"

"A really cute coward, but still. Coward." He pointed at her, and she grabbed his finger.

"Quit it. I am not. Anyway, coward, what was wrong with *you* asking *me*?" she retorted.

"Don't break my finger. You already broke my nose, and if you break my hand I won't be able to work the rest of the summer," Paul joked. "And then how would you cut the lemons correctly?"

"You could still come to work and tell me how to do everything — you know, kind of like you already do," Holly said.

"Harsh! I was only trying to help," Paul said. He stepped closer and swept at a piece of fire extinguisher foam in her hair. Then he didn't let go. He leaned closer to her, putting his arms around her waist, and said, "You know what?"

Holly felt like she was going to burst with happiness as she looked up at him. "What?"

"Your hair smells *really* smoky."

She swatted him on the ear. "Yours, too!" Holly said. "Like . . . campfire smoky."

"But it's still really pretty," he continued, running one hand through her hair. "Too bad you hate working with me so much."

"It is too bad. It's horrible," she said, standing on her tiptoes and closing her eyes to kiss him.

Holly had never had a real kiss before. Now she understood why her sisters had told her that you couldn't explain what was so good about it — it just *was*.

Suddenly there was a loud squeaking sound,

and Holly broke away from the kiss to look up. Several firefighters in tall black boots were marching toward the kitchen.

"We hate to interrupt you, but we hear there's a fire?" a firefighter standing almost right next to them asked.

"Uh, yes. Yes, sir." This time, Paul was the one who turned red with embarrassment.

"Seems to be mostly out now. Care to explain what happened?" the firefighter asked.

Together they followed him over to the kitchen.

"Who's telling Russell?" Holly whispered to Paul.

Paul pointed to their manager, who was running across the patio at top speed. "Looks like he's already been told."

Russell stopped and took one glance at the kitchen. "Good. Maybe *now* she'll agree we need a new stove," he muttered as he flipped open his cell phone and called Mrs. Whittingham.

"'*Good*'?" Holly said, and she and Paul cracked up laughing.

The patio was filling with people coming to check out the noise and smoke.

"What happened?" Ainslee cried as she

walked up to Holly, with Ross right behind her. "We were playing tennis and all of a sudden I heard sirens —"

"Are you guys hurt?" Ross asked.

"No, we're, uh, fine." Holly glanced at Paul and smiled, as Ainslee leaned in to give her a quick hug.

"We got out just in time," Paul said.

"Paul, could you come help us out for a second?" Russell asked. "We need to make a report to the fire crew."

As Paul and Russell headed off, Holly looked at Ainslee and for the first time noticed something drastic had changed about her.

"Hey, Ross? Do you think you could find me a bottled water?" Holly asked. "My throat's kind of parched."

"Oh, yeah — of course. Be right back," Ross promised.

As soon as He was gone, Holly pointed to the pale pink terry-cloth headband around Ainslee's forehead. "Excuse me, what's that?"

"I couldn't find my visor, so I was wearing this. Is it okay?" asked Ainslee. "I got it at the pro shop; there was a sale. Does it look all right? Because I think it matches my skirt, but my shirt, I don't know." She glanced down at her silver-gray tennis skirt and silver-blue tank top.

"Why don't you ask Ross? He's the headband king," Holly said. "Right?" She looked at Ainslee for verification, but all of a sudden Ainslee was acting like she'd never heard the term before, much less invented it.

"Wait a second," Holly said. "Do you not hate the fact he wears headbands now?"

"Headbands aren't so bad. I mean, he does look pretty good in them," Ainslee said. "And if he has his own thing, then that's cool, right?" She glanced around the patio. "I wonder what's taking him so long. But, anyway, I've been dying to tell you. Right after I talked to you last night, he called me to ask me to that party! And I started thinking about what my mom was saying all the time. Like, how the best thing could be right under your nose. Or next to your court. And there's Ross, you know? And we totally have everything in common."

"Like your matching headbands," Holly interrupted.

"Shut up. They're not *matching*," Ainslee said, swatting her arm. "Mine's pink, plus it's a girl size, plus —"

"Right. You know, I think he's been interested in you for a while," Holly said.

"And you didn't tell me?" Ainslee demanded.

"Well, at first I wasn't sure because he's so laid-back all the time, and because all he ever talked about was your *game*."

"I know, isn't it cool?" Ainslee replied. "He's, like, my number one fan. Anyway, I have you to thank, because Ross said you encouraged him to call me last night."

"Yeah, well, I did, but I kind of had mixed motives," Holly admitted. "Even though I said I didn't want to ask Paul? I really did."

"Yeah, I kind of got that when I talked to you. That whole you-protest-too-much vibe."

"How *Midsummer Night* of you," Holly teased.

Ainslee was bouncing on the toes of her tennis shoes. "Oh my God. So *did* you ask him?"

"Not last night, because I thought *you* were. But today the fire kind of got us talking, and then —" Holly spotted Ross coming from the kitchen, beside Paul. "Here they come. I'll give you the details later. The bottom line is — yes!"

"Wow. Quelle excitement around here these days," Ainslee said as they walked up.

Ross handed Holly a bottled water, then gave one to Ainslee, too. "I thought maybe you were thirsty after that last set," he said.

"Wait a second. You guys were playing?" Holly asked.

"Well, yeah. That's why I came in early," Ainslee said. "We've got to seriously start practicing if we want to win that tournament. Glad you guys are okay, but we've got to go."

Holly smiled as they headed off across the patio, toward the courts on the other side of the club. "Très interesting," she muttered as she watched them walk side by side.

"So I have good news and bad news," Paul said. "The good news is that the kitchen is actually okay. The bad news is that we have to go back to work."

"We can't take a pool break while Russell cleans up?" asked Holly.

"Not exactly. He's getting out the cleaning products for us, while he goes appliance shopping."

"Oh. Well, why don't we go start, and you can tell me how to clean," Holly suggested, heading inside.

"Shut up," Paul said, laughing as he chased her into the kitchen.

"How can it be a romantic Midsummer Night Party when it's not the middle of the summer, and it's only eight and not even dark yet?" Ainslee complained as they sat outside the country club.

They were all seated at a table under a large white tent, where all the party guests were eating, mingling, and talking.

"And the music is, like . . . historical?" Ross added.

Mrs. Whittingham had hired a big band for the occasion. They seemed to know only music from her childhood.

"This tent looks a hundred years old, too. If there's a slight breeze tonight, I bet it'll collapse," Holly said.

"Anyone for more Retro-ade?" Paul offered as he stood.

Ainslee laughed. "Sounds delish, but no thanks. But could you bring back some of those little chocolate éclair thingies?"

"I'll come with you and help," Holly said, standing up. "We're not really getting Retro-ade, are we?" she asked as she and Paul headed to the buffet table.

"No. Some of those shrimp puffs, maybe."

Paul took her hand and gently nudged her in another direction. "Come on, let's go around front."

"Why?" asked Holly.

"To be alone for a second," Paul said. They walked to the club's entrance, where the fountain was lit by white lights that were supposed to be synchronized to the water flow, but were off by a few seconds.

"Look at that thing too long and you get dizzy," Holly noticed.

"So don't look." Paul pulled her closer to him, and she leaned her head on his chest, snuggling a little. "You want to dance?" he asked softly.

"Sure, but —"

Just then the fountain burst like a miniature Old Faithful, drenching the two of them in a shower of water. Holly shrieked and jumped away, but her hair and dress were semisoaked by the time she did. Paul's face was wet, and his shirt looked like he'd been caught in a downpour.

They started laughing. "What is wrong with this place!" Holly cried, giggling. "Is it us?"

"No, it's not us. It's *you*," Paul said.

"Oh, really?" Holly pushed against Paul's arms, trying to shove him into the fountain.

"What are you —" He struggled against her.

As they were wrestling, the fountain misfired again, spraying them, and they both fell laughing into its pool of water.

"Swim much?" Paul asked, pushing Holly's wet hair back behind her ears.

"Shut up," Holly said, as she leaned forward to kiss him.

Do you 💗 bikinis, too?

Try these two on for size!

From HE'S WITH ME
by Tamara Summers

"Can't you just say no?" Colin asked Jake.

"Even I know the answer to that," Lexie said. "Nobody says no to Bree." Lexie understood exactly what Jake was worried about. She'd been avoiding Bree since elementary school. If you stayed far under her radar, you could slip by unnoticed and unharmed, but if you popped into her line of sight in any way, she would rip you to shreds with one flick of her French-tipped nails.

"Doomed," Jake muttered. "Dooooomed."

"All right," Colin said. "Tell her you already have a girlfriend."

Jake thought for a minute. "Like, long distance? I don't think she'll buy that. Plus it's only been a week since school ended. Where would I have picked up a girlfriend in a week?"

"I dunno." Colin shrugged. "You could tell her you're dating Lexie."

Lexie was so, so, SO glad that Colin had his eyes glued to the camera controls and didn't see her expression. Jake kept his arms over his face, so he didn't notice, either. She felt like she might faint. There was a really awkward pause, and Lexie wondered if she was supposed to make a joke here.

She started to say, "As if — " at the same time as Jake said, "Well, I — " and they both stopped.

"What were you going to say?" he said. He put his arms down and tilted his head back to look at her.

"Um, just . . . as if she'll believe that."

"Why?" Colin said. Lexie wished Jake would say something, but he just kept looking at her.

"Well, if you think Bree is out of his league, then I'm in another solar system, aren't I?" she tried to joke.

"Actually, it might work," Jake said. Lexie bit her tongue, she was so surprised.

"Sure it will," Colin said. "Lexie will be at Summerlodge, too, so Bree can see you're together. And it's only for a little while, until Bree gets over you. And it's not like there's anyone Lexie wants to date, so you're hardly putting a dent in her love life. Right, Lexie?"

That's nice. Thanks, Colin.

"What do you say, Lexie?" Jake said, rolling over onto his stomach and propping his elbows on the floor and his chin in his hands adorably. "Want to be my pretend girlfriend?" His eyes were like storm clouds, big and unstoppable and irresistible.

Lexie, this is what you've been dreaming about.

Correction: This is a strange parody of what you've been dreaming about. Is this really what you want? Being Jake's pretend girlfriend?

Yeah, sure, okay. Close enough!

"Okay," she said, feeling dizzy. "I mean, it'll be tough pretending to like you, but I guess I can take one for the team. Right?"

"You're my knight in shining armor," Jake said, getting up and kneeling on the couch next to her. Right next to her. "My hero, my warrior princess," he said, taking her hand. "My King Kong." He pressed her hand to his heart. She could actually feel it beating through the soft fabric of his shirt. It was going really fast. Nearly as fast as hers, but he was an athlete, so it probably went that fast all the time.

"Okay, here are the Rules of Pretend Dating Lexie," she said. "You need to STOP comparing me to a giant gorilla."

"What are the other rules?" he asked. He was still holding her hand against his chest.

"That's the only one," she said. Was her voice shaking? Could he tell? "So far. I'll keep you posted as others come up."

He grinned. "I'll look forward to it."

"Okay," Colin said, standing up. "I think I've figured out how to change it to night recording. Let's go test it in the shed." He picked up a flashlight and headed for the stairs. Lexie couldn't believe her own twin hadn't noticed how much she was blushing. She wanted to stay where she was forever, but she pulled her hand free and scrambled off the couch.

"Great, okay," she said. "Sounds like fun." She looked back from the doorway. "Coming, Jake?"

"You bet," he said, standing up and stretching. "Where my girlfriend goes, I go."

Lexie shivered.

I always thought my first boyfriend would be Jake. But I never thought it would only be pretend. . . .

From ISLAND SUMMER
by Jeanine Le Ny

"So, I guess you're delivering sandwiches," the guy piped up.

"Huh? Oh. Right. Uh-huh. Maybe you want to order one sometime. I'm sure there's a menu around here somewhere," Nikki replied, fully aware that she was now babbling. She began to search the pile of sandwiches and found a flyer at the bottom. As she tugged at it, a hoagie toppled out of the basket.

"Whoa!" The boy tried to catch it, but it fell to the sidewalk with a splat.

That was when Nikki noticed he was holding a

leash, which was attached to a tiny orange Pomeranian, which now had a big yellowish-brown squirt of honey mustard matting the fur on top of its head.

The boy laughed. "Aunt Winnie is not going to be happy about that."

"Oops!" Nikki threw the leaky sandwich back into the bicycle basket, grabbed a pile of napkins, and attempted to wipe off the dog as it yapped and nipped at her fingers. "Sorry!"

"Forget it," the boy said, crouching down and taking the napkins from Nikki. As he did this he smiled and Nikki smiled back, feeling a weird and exciting energy ping back and forth between them. Her stomach suddenly felt as if a hundred butterflies had decided to get together for a game of tag in there.

"Well, I've got to get Button back to my aunt," the boy said, gesturing to the Pomeranian and turning to leave.

"Wait!" Nikki cried a little too loudly. She hoped that it didn't come off as slightly psycho.

The boy turned back and Nikki handed him the menu. "You forgot this," she said. Then, in a bold move, she added, "My name's Nikki, by the way. What's yours?"

"Daniel," he said.

Not knowing what else to do, Nikki casually gazed back into the window of the nail salon, where the women inside seemed to have lost interest, thank God. She waited a few seconds to see if Daniel had anything to ask her. Like maybe if he could have her number or something.

Daniel sort of coughed and shoved his hands into the pockets of his enormous camouflage shorts.

Why isn't he asking? Nikki waited a few more seconds. *Maybe he's shy*, she told herself. *Maybe you should just ask HIM for HIS number.*

Why not? This WAS the twenty-first century, after all. Okay. She'd go for it. In three . . . two . . . one. . . .

"Um, Daniel, I . . . I . . ." I can't do it! she thought, chickening out. ". . . I guess I'd better finish my deliveries. . . ." She paused, giving him a chance to talk.

"Oh. Right. No problem," he said, walking backward. "It was really nice meeting you, Nikki." He tripped over Button's leash but recovered nicely. "Heh, heh." He grinned nervously and waved. "Bye, Nikki."

She liked the way he said her name a lot. "Bye."

Nikki smiled again and waved as Daniel headed down Main Street with Button. She really wished she'd had the nerve to get his number. He was so adorable and sweet. She wouldn't mind seeing him again. No, she wouldn't mind it at all.

To Do List: Read all the Point books!

By Aimee Friedman

☐ **South Beach**
0-439-70678-5

☐ **French Kiss**
0-439-79281-9

☐ **Hollywood Hills**
0-439-79282-7

By Hailey Abbott

☐ **Summer Boys**
0-439-54020-8

☐ **Next Summer: A Summer Boys Novel**
0-439-75540-9

☐ **After Summer: A Summer Boys Novel**
0-439-86367-8

☐ **Last Summer: A Summer Boys Novel**
0-439-86725-8

By Claudia Gabel

☐ **In or Out**
0-439-91853-7

By Nina Malkin

☐ **6X: The Uncensored Confessions**
0-439-72421-X

☐ **6X: Loud, Fast, & Out of Control**
0-439-72422-8

☐ **Orange Is the New Pink**
0-439-89965-6

POINTCKLT